The Case of the Natty Newfie

A Thousand Islands Doggy Inn Mystery

B.R. Snow

Copyright © 2017 B.R. Snow

ISBN: 978-1-942691-41-9

Website: www.brsnow.net/

Twitter:@BernSnow

Facebook: facebook.com/bernsnow

Cover Design: Reggie Cullen

Cover Photo: James R. Miller

Other Books by B.R. Snow

The Thousand Islands Doggy Inn Mysteries

- The Case of the Abandoned Aussie
- The Case of the Brokenhearted Bulldog
- The Case of the Caged Cockers
- The Case of the Dapper Dandie Dinmont
- The Case of the Eccentric Elkhound
- The Case of the Faithful Frenchie
- The Case of the Graceful Goldens
- The Case of the Hurricane Hounds
- The Case of the Itinerant Ibizan
- The Case of the Jaded Jack Russell
- The Case of the Klutzy King Charles
- The Case of the Lovable Labs
- The Case of the Mellow Maltese

The Whiskey Run Chronicles

- Episode 1 – The Dry Season Approaches
- Episode 2 – Friends and Enemies
- Episode 3 – Let the Games Begin
- Episode 4 – Enter the Revenuer
- Episode 5 – A Changing Landscape
- Episode 6 – Entrepreneurial Spirits
- Episode 7 – All Hands On Deck
- The Whiskey Run Chronicles – The Complete Volume 1

The Damaged Posse

- American Midnight
- Larrikin Gene
- Sneaker World
- Summerman
- The Duplicates

Other Books

- Divorce Hotel
- Either Ore

To Laurie and Stella

Chapter 1

The Immigration agent handed our passports to me through the window then glanced into the back seat where Chef Claire was surrounded by four dogs who were all eager to introduce themselves. Chef Claire lowered the window, and the dogs clamored over her and surged forward to greet him. Captain, Josie's massive Newfie, beat the others to the punch and stuck his head through the window to say hello the laughing man.

"And how about you?" the agent said to Captain. "Where's your passport?"

Captain woofed once, and his tail smacked Chef Claire in the face twice, once in each direction, before she was able to get a hand up to defend herself.

"Hey," Chef Claire said, grudgingly giving up room in the back seat. "I'm sitting here."

The agent rubbed Captain's head then made time for my Australian Shepherd, Chloe, and Chef Claire's Goldens, Al and Dente. Then he refocused on me behind the wheel.

"That's a good-looking bunch of dogs you've got there," he said.

"Thanks," I said. "We like to think so."

"I'll just need to see their papers," the agent said.

Josie leaned over from the passenger seat and handed them to him. He flipped through the documents and handed them back through the window.

"Hey, now I recognize you folks," he said, nodding. "You run the Doggy Inn over in Clay Bay."

"Guilty as charged," I said, smiling at him.

"And you have that restaurant with the amazing chef, right?"

"Aren't you sweet," Chef Claire said.

"That's the amazing one in the backseat," I said.

"My wife and I had dinner there just last week. It was incredible," he said, poking his head through the window to speak to Chef Claire. "We both had a pasta dish. Pesto with chicken."

"Good call," Josie said, nodding.

"Was that a bit of bacon I tasted in the pesto?" he said.

"Actually, it was Jamon Iberico de Bellota ham," Chef Claire said.

"What's the difference?" he said, frowning.

"About sixty bucks a pound," Chef Claire said, laughing. Then she focused on Josie. "And last night I just happened to notice that a huge chunk of it is missing."

"We probably have mice," Josie said, glancing over her shoulder.

"What's the purpose of your trip to Canada today?"

"We have a meeting in Ottawa," I said.

"A photo shoot," Josie said. "Actually, it's the dogs' photo shoot."

"I see," he said, reaching through the back window again to pet both Goldens. "Famous dogs, huh?"

"Not yet," I said, laughing. "We're getting ready to launch our new dog toy company, and we're going to use the dogs in some of the marketing materials. That is if we can get them to sit still long enough."

"Dog toy company?" he said, nodding. "Nice. Okay, you better get going then. I wouldn't want to make them late for their closeup. Drive safe and take good care of these guys."

"Will do. Thanks."

He stepped back from the car, gave me a quick wave and focused on the car behind us. I raised the window and slowly accelerated. Captain and Chloe clamored over the seat and stretched out in the back of the SUV. Al and Dente remained in the back seat draped across Chef Claire's lap. A few minutes later, it started snowing, and I glanced over at Josie.

"Do you see that?" I said, nodding at the windshield.

"I'm sure it's just a flurry," Josie said. "It's too early in the season for it to stick, right?"

"Yeah, I'm sure it is," I said, frowning. "Don't you think?"

"Probably," she said, glancing out the window at the snow that was beginning to fall harder.

"Oh, I forgot to tell you," Chef Claire said. "I talked with your mom last night, and she wants to go over the menu for

Thanksgiving dinner. I thought we'd just do it during family dinner night on Monday."

"That works," I said, glancing at her through the rearview mirror. "Does she have a number yet?"

"She said over a hundred and fifty have confirmed so far," Chef Claire said. "But it's going to go up."

"Where are we going to put everybody?" I said.

"I think we might have to add a second seating," Chef Claire said. "We could do one at noon and then another around four."

"How much extra work is that going to be for you and the staff?" Josie said, turning around in her seat.

"A bit," she said, shrugging. "But we'll make it work."

This was going to be our second year providing dinner to local residents who were on their own during Thanksgiving or were elderly and no longer capable of cooking for themselves. Like so many community activities in our little town of Clay Bay, this one had been the brainchild of my mother. And like most of her other ideas, it had been a major success.

"I want to be assigned dessert duty this year," Josie said. "Last year, I was on gravy detail and made a real mess."

"Yes, we noticed," Chef Claire said.

"I still say there was something wrong with that ladle," Josie said, glancing over her shoulder. Then she looked over at me. "Is Abby going to meet us at the photo shoot?"

"She is," I said. "And she's bringing her two Springer Spaniels."

"Great," Josie said. "I've been dying to meet them. Between the six of them, we should be able to get some good shots we can use."

Abby Vandenburgh is our new CEO of Wags, the dog toy company we acquired several months ago. The woman who had invented the line of dog toys had a very short stint as our original CEO, but then she was arrested as an accomplice in a murder her brother had committed. Although she still holds a twenty-percent stake in the company, she is currently serving a long prison sentence courtesy of the Canadian judicial system. The fact that her brother, now serving a life sentence, was also an ex-boyfriend of Chef Claire had made our acquisition of the fledgling company even stranger. But after several months of start-up activities, including the build-out of the manufacturing facility and the hiring of three dozen staff, we were finally ready to launch.

"Who's the photographer?" Chef Claire said.

"Thomas recommended him," I said. "Apparently, they're buddies. Thomas is going to meet us at the shoot. And after that, he wants to give us a tour of the factory."

"I can't believe this is actually happening," Josie said.

"Yeah, look at us," I said, laughing. "Dog toy magnates."

"So, where is this guy's studio located?" Josie said.

"According to Thomas, he has a downtown loft, and that's where he does most of his work," I said.

"And you're sure that Max is okay with us staying at his place?" Josie said.

"Absolutely," I said, nodding. "In fact, he insisted."

Max is my new boyfriend, and I have to admit that I'm excited about my first trip to Ottawa since we started dating a few months ago. He's visited me in Clay Bay three times, and it's my turn to make the two-hour drive. I have a feeling that this is just the first in a long series of trips I'll be making across the border.

"Don't worry," Josie said with an evil grin. "We promise to make ourselves scarce and do our best not to listen."

"Speak for yourself," Chef Claire said from the backseat.

"Shut it," I said, my face turning red. I glanced through the rearview mirror. "It's awfully quiet back there. What are the bruisers doing?"

"They're all sacked out," Chef Claire said. "Don't look now, but the snow is starting to accumulate."

"It is," I said. "It's pretty."

"I hope we get a foot," Chef Claire said.

"Bite your tongue," Josie said.

"I wouldn't mind going cross country skiing a few times before we head to Cayman," she said.

Josie and I both snorted.

"Well, I like it," Chef Claire said. "It makes me feel alive."

6

"So does breathing," Josie said.

"Good point," I said, glancing over at her.

"Thank you," she said, reaching into her bag. "Bite-sized?"

"Don't mind if I do," I said, grabbing a small handful from the bag she was holding out.

She passed the bag to Chef Claire, and I was about to unwrap one of the chocolate delights when I paused and tossed it into the cup holder next to me.

"Wow," I said, slowing down. "Where the heck did this come from?"

It was evident that we were now heading directly into a major snowstorm, and about three inches had already accumulated on the highway.

"Ottawa must be getting pounded," Josie said. "We should have checked the forecast before we left."

"It came out of nowhere," I said, slowing down to forty. I reached into my bag and grabbed my phone. I dialed the number and set the phone in its dashboard holder. "Hey, Thomas. It's Suzy."

"Hey, where are you guys?" he said.

"We're about forty miles out, but we just hit a huge storm. How much are you getting there?"

"Six inches and counting," Thomas said. "Take it easy on the way in. It looks like the plows are just getting out."

"Will do," I said, focusing on the road and the city traffic that was already starting to build. "You want to call the photographer and tell him we might be a bit late?"

"No, that's not necessary. I'm already here," Thomas said. "And so is Abby."

"Hi, Suzy," our new CEO said through the phone.

"Hey, we're probably about an hour out. Maybe a bit more."

"Take your time," Abby said. "We're just sitting here drinking coffee and watching the snow fall."

"It's way too early for a major storm," I said. "Did you bring your Springers?"

"I did," she said. "And they're dying to go outside and play in the snow."

"Maybe we can get some shots of all the dogs outside later," I said.

"That's a great idea," Abby said. "Hang on a sec."

I heard a sidebar conversation on the other end of the phone. Then she came back on the line.

"John said you should park in the structure underneath his building. There's guest parking on the second level. If you park on the street, you might not be able to find your car later if it keeps snowing like this."

"That's not funny," I said, grimacing at the thought of having to deal with knee-high snow this early in the season.

"I wish I could tell you that funny was what I was going for," she said, laughing. "Drive safe."

"See you soon."

I ended the call and continued to stare out at the traffic that had slowed even further. The visibility was dreadful, and I shook my head.

"It looks like you might get your wish," I said to Chef Claire through the mirror.

"I should have brought my skis," Chef Claire said, leaning forward to look out through the windshield.

"Where is Max's place compared to where the photographer is located?" Josie said.

"I don't think it's too far," I said. "Why?"

"Because if the plows don't make it out soon, we might end up having to hoof it," Josie said.

"Walk to Max's in knee-high snow with four dogs?" I said, glancing over at her with a raised eyebrow. "Not gonna happen."

Josie and Chef Claire both laughed.

"Laugh all you want," I said, glancing back and forth at them. "I'm not joking."

Chapter 2

A little over an hour later, we made it into downtown Ottawa, and the overall scene, while not chaotic, was a complete mess. The first snowstorm of the year has a tendency to catch many people off guard, and it was obvious that this year would be no different. Several drivers who hadn't gotten around to putting winter tires on their cars were spinning their wheels on the half-foot of unplowed snow and sliding into the turns they were trying to make. Other drivers, those unaccustomed to driving in the snow I assumed, were either going too fast or slamming their brakes instead of slowly pumping them when needed. We watched a sedan lose control going through an intersection and slide sideways into a truck that was waiting for a red light to turn, and I barely managed to make it around both vehicles just as the drivers climbed out to examine the damage.

I white-knuckled my way down a side street, turned onto Kent Street, then got very lucky and ended up behind a snowplow that was making short work of the accumulation on our side of the street. I followed the plow for about a mile, then made the turn that led to the photographer's building. A few minutes later, I maneuvered the SUV into the parking garage and came to a gentle stop in one of the guest parking spots. I turned the vehicle off and realized my breathing pattern had become irregular and my fingers cramped. All four dogs began to stir in the back.

"Good job," Josie said. "It's nasty out there."

"It's been a while since I've driven in snow like this," I said, reaching for my bag.

"And?" Josie said, grinning.

"And I haven't missed it one bit," I said. "Okay, it looks like the elevator is off to our right. He's on the fifth floor. You guys ready?"

"Let me just get the bruisers' leads on them," Chef Claire said.

"Uh-oh," Josie said.

"What?"

"They're probably going to need to pee first."

"Yeah, you're right," I said, glancing out the window. "Well, there's no way we can walk them back down the entrance ramp."

"No, that would be too dangerous," Josie said. "But a lot of the residents here must have pets, right?"

"I'd be shocked if they didn't."

"Let's take the elevator to the lobby," Josie said. "There must be a courtyard or something like that off the main floor."

"Good plan," I said, then looked at Chef Claire. "Are you all set?"

"Let's do this," she said. "You guys get out and take a door. I'll hand you two leads each."

11

"Got it," I said, climbing out of the car. I opened one of the back doors, and Chef Claire handed me the leads attached to Al and Dente. Both Goldens effortlessly hopped out of the car and sat quietly at my feet. "Look at these two," I said, amazed by how well they'd been trained. "Who's the good dogs?"

Captain and Chloe, apparently worried they were either going to be left behind in the car or that they were missing something, scrambled around in the back seat and ended up and draped across Chef Claire's lap with their leads tangled.

"Smooth," Josie said, shaking her head at both of them. "Chef Claire, why don't you get out and grab your guys? Suzy and I will see if we can get Null and Void out of the car without them strangling themselves."

Chef Claire laughed and slid out from underneath Captain and Chloe. I handed her both leads then leaned into the backseat and untangled the leads. I handed Captain's to Josie then waited for Chloe to hop down out of the car, her tail wagging furiously. I closed the back door, waited for Josie to do the same, then locked the car. We headed for the elevator with the dogs leading the way and soon found ourselves in the lobby. We ended up there because that was the only floor the elevator from the parking garage stopped on. I noticed a security guard sitting nearby behind a desk and approached him.

"Hi," I said, holding Chloe's lead tight as she strained to get closer to the guard to say hello.

"Look at these guys," the security guard said, getting up out of his chair to greet the dogs. "They're gorgeous."

"Thanks," I said. "We have an appointment with John Naylor, but these guys need to take care of a little business first."

"Sure," he said, kneeling down to rub Chloe's head. "She's an Aussie shepherd, right?"

"She is," I said, releasing the tension on her lead. "How much snow are they predicting?"

"This morning they were talking about only a dusting," he said, turning his attention to Captain. "Now, they're saying we might end up breaking the record."

"What's the record?" Josie said.

"I think it's around fifty centimeters," the guard said, rubbing the Newfie's head.

I frowned. Josie caught my expression and laughed.

"That's around two feet," she said.

"I knew that," I said, making a face at her. "Is it okay if we take them out to that courtyard?"

"That's the spot," the guard said. "You'll find plastic gloves and baggies outside the door if you need them."

"Thanks," I said, glancing outside at the snow that continued to fall and was now swirling in the breeze. "Okay, let's get this over with."

We headed outside with the dogs, and Al and Dente immediately focused on the task at hand, and within a few minutes, Chef Claire was back inside the warm building laughing and chatting with the security guard. Captain and Chloe decided that rolling around in the snow and having a wrestling match sounded like a good idea, and Josie and I stood shivering in the cold until they finally found their focus. Eventually, they left their mark in the snow, and we were able to get them to shake off, and we headed back inside.

"When are we going to Cayman?" Josie said, stamping snow off her feet.

"Not soon enough," I said, hugging myself for warmth. "I can't believe I used to look forward to this time of year." I glanced at Chef Claire. "Are we all set?"

"We are," she said, pointing at a bank of elevators.

We waved to the security guard then stepped into the elevator. The dogs sat quietly as the door closed and we began our ascent.

"It looks like you made a friend," Josie said to Chef Claire.

"The security guard? He was nice," she said. "And a treasure trove of information."

"Really?" Josie said. "Do tell."

"Well, apparently, our photographer has quite a reputation," she said, giving us a coy smile.

"Let me guess," I said. "But not as a dog photographer."

"Nothing gets past you," Chef Claire said. "He likes to call himself a *portrait* photographer."

"I assume you're not talking about Norman Rockwell," Josie said.

14

"No, more like rock *star*," Chef Claire said. "And models. Lots of models. The security guard said he sees women going in and out all the time. Rumor has it that the guy is a bit of a player."

"I guess everybody has got to make a living, right?" I said, shrugging. "And I'm sure he'll be on his best behavior today."

"He's one of Thomas's buddies?" Josie said.

"Yeah, that's what he said," I said. "I think they go clubbing together."

"Hey, they're young," Josie said. "That's what young people do. You remember what those days were like, don't you?"

"Barely," I said, laughing as the elevator came to a stop on the fifth floor.

"But that's not all he does," Chef Claire said.

I paused in the open doorway and waited for Chef Claire to continue.

"Apparently, he moonlights as one of the local paparazzi," she said. "Several of his photos have shown up in the tabloids and websites focused on celebrities."

"But not photos highlighting their charity work, right?" I said.

"Man, you're on fire today," Josie said, laughing.

"Shut it," I said, making a face at her. "So, this guy is a total sleazeball?"

"No, actually, the guard said he's a really nice guy," Chef Claire said. "But he definitely has an eye for the ladies. And he also considers himself an entrepreneur."

"That's probably a good thing," Josie said, taking in her surroundings as we led the dogs down the hall toward his loft. "It must cost a small fortune to live here."

We came to a stop outside the door, and Josie pressed the buzzer. Moments later, Thomas opened the door and beamed at us.

"You made it," he said, giving us room to enter. "How bad is it out there?"

"It's getting nasty," I said, giving him a hug. "It's good to see you. How's it going?"

"Things are great," he said. "Let me take your coats."

We handed them to him, and he headed for a long line of metal hooks attached to one of the walls near the door.

"Hey, guys."

"Hi, Abby," I said, giving our CEO a warm embrace. "How are you doing?"

"Terrific," she said, then nodded at a young man at the far end of the loft I assumed was the photographer. "You're not going to believe this kid."

"Really? So, the rumors are true," I said, scowling.

"It's okay," Abby said, laughing. "He's just young and a bit of a flirt." She bent down to greet all four of our dogs just as two

16

beautiful Springer Spaniels came bounding across the floor. "And these two are Bert and Ernie."

Josie and I sat down on the floor to say hello to the Springers and ended up rolling around on the floor with all six dogs. We eventually got to our feet when the photographer strolled toward us trailed by a young woman. He was in his early twenties, and his goofy grin seemed etched in place. The woman with him was also young and smiling, but every move she made seemed tentative, and for some reason, she reminded me of a fragile baby bird.

"I'm John Naylor," he said, smiling and giving all three of us the once-over. "And this is my assistant, Melinda." He sat down on the floor and greeted the dogs then almost disappeared from view when Captain placed a huge paw on his shoulder and pinned him on the floor.

"It's nice to meet you," I said, extending my hand toward the young blonde who was obviously a dog lover. "I'm Suzy. That's Josie. And that's Chef Claire."

"Welcome," Melinda said, returning our handshakes with a big smile before giving her undivided attention to both Goldens. "These guys are incredible."

"Thanks," Chef Claire said, petting the two Springers. "How old are your guys?"

"They're two," Abby said. "And finally starting to settle down."

Thomas returned, and John climbed to his feet and brushed himself off. That seemed to be unnecessary since the place was immaculate. The fact that a young man in his early twenties kept such a tidy home caught me by surprise.

"You guys want something to drink?" John Naylor said. "I just made a big pot of coffee."

"That sounds good," Josie said.

As we followed him toward the kitchen that dominated the middle of the loft, I got my first good look at the place. It appeared to be about the size of a basketball court, and the dark hardwood floor was polished to a high sheen. The back quarter of the loft where I assumed he did most of his photo shoots was already set up for our session. The living room area was near the kitchen, and another section I assumed to be the bedroom was cordoned off by an elaborate set of Japanese screens. I continued to take it all in then looked over at Josie who was doing the same.

"This place is amazing," Josie said.

"Yeah, it's gorgeous," I said, nodding. "The kid has great taste."

"Either that or a really good decorator," Chef Claire said. "I love the kitchen."

The photographer noticed us admiring the loft as he began setting fresh mugs of coffee on the counter that ran along the front of the kitchen.

"I love it here," he said, glancing around.

"I'd be shocked if you didn't," Josie said. "What do these lofts rent for?"

"I think they go for about five grand a month," he said, frowning. "But I'm not really sure. I bought this one."

He saw the look of surprise on all our faces and grinned.

"Yeah, I know," he said. "I get that all the time. How is it possible for a kid like me to buy a place like this?"

"You read my mind," Josie said, stirring her coffee and taking a sip. "Business must be good."

"It better be," John said, laughing. "I've got a monthly nut that could choke a horse." Then he shrugged. "But what the heck, right? If you're not working hard, you're not trying." Then he noticed the look on my face. "What is it?"

"Given the size of your monthly nut, I was just wondering what you're charging us," I said, laughing.

"We were just discussing that when you guys got here," Abby said. "John has offered to do the shoot and the initial marketing campaign for free if we're willing to give him a cut of the first-year revenue."

"Interesting," I said, remembering what the security guard had told Chef Claire about his entrepreneurial spirit. "How much of a cut are you thinking about?"

"Abby said your first-year revenue target is around five million," John said.

"That sounds about right," I said, glancing at Abby who confirmed it with a nod.

19

"No offense, but I think it's way too low," he said, taking a sip of his coffee. "I got a good look at your dog toys this morning, and they're incredible. And with the distribution deal you have with Middleton Enterprises, combined with what I think you'll be able to do online, your first-year revenue should be higher. If you only did five million, I'd be very disappointed. That is if I were you."

"The margins on five million are nothing to sneeze at," Abby said, an edginess creeping into her voice.

"Not at all," John said, casually topping off everyone's coffee. "But why be happy with five when you can do ten?"

"Ten million?" I said, raising an eyebrow at him.

"It's very doable," he said, nodding his head vigorously. "And it should ramp up to at least fifty million in year two."

I had no idea where his confidence came from, and I was both mildly annoyed and impressed by his cockiness.

"What do you know about the pet industry?" I said.

"Not much," he said, shaking his head. "But I know a lot about putting together ad and marketing campaigns. And I know a winner when I see it. This thing could be huge."

"We think so," I said. "And that's why we hired Abby."

"And that was a very smart decision on your part," John said. "Not to mention what a great call it was hiring this guy to handle your logistics." He draped an arm over Thomas's shoulder. "But you're very thin at the moment on the marketing side."

"We have Middleton Enterprises to handle most of that," I said.

"On the retail side, sure," John said. "But your idea of doing an online subscription service for the toys is brilliant."

"Thanks," I said.

"That's a billion-dollar idea," John said. "If it's designed and executed well."

"I'm listening," I said, folding my arms and leaning back against the counter.

"Okay, let's start with the size of the dog market. It's around sixteen billion a year in the States."

"But that's all in," Josie said. "And it includes veterinary services and all sorts of ancillary items."

"Yeah, I get that," John said, nodding. "But I just read where dog owners spend over a hundred bucks a year on average for toys and treats. And there are about eighty million dogs in the U.S. alone. So, let's be really conservative and take out strays, shelter dogs, and poor guys like that and say there are around fifty million dogs that people spend a hundred bucks a year on for discretionary items. That alone is a five-billion-dollar market. Ten percent market share of that is five hundred million."

"We're very familiar with the numbers, John," Abby said.

"I'm sure you are," he said, shrugging. "And I'm also sure your business plan is a lot more precise than the numbers I'm tossing off the top of my head. I'm just saying you guys should ramp up your projected revenues a lot faster than what you're currently planning. With my help, I think you can grow this thing to three hundred million annually by year five."

"I thought you were a photographer," I said, laughing as I found myself warming up to him despite his annoying cockiness that was off the charts.

"I am. Photography is my passion," he said. "I just have a knack for marketing." He took a sip of coffee and beamed at us. "And I also have a knack for making money."

"So, I repeat. How much of a cut are you thinking about?" I said, glancing back and forth at Josie and Chef Claire who were listening closely to the conversation.

"Here's my offer," he said, setting his coffee mug down. "I'll do the photo shoot and develop all the marketing materials and design your website for the cost of materials. It shouldn't be more than ten grand tops. And I get two percent of the first five million, your first-year target."

"A hundred thousand?" I said.

"Well done," Josie whispered. "And you didn't even need to take your shoes off."

"Shut it," I said, grinning at her.

"It's a lot cheaper than hiring a senior VP of marketing," John said.

"No argument there," Abby said.

"And I get five percent of everything in excess of your annual sales targets," John said, holding up the coffee pot to see if anyone wanted more.

I waved the offer away as I tried processing the numbers involved. I glanced at Abby who was also deep in thought.

"So, for every million bucks in revenue over our annual target you get fifty thousand?" I said.

"That's my offer," he said, smiling. "Subject to negotiation, of course. And if I do get you guys to ten million in year one, our deal continues for another two years at the same percentages."

"You've given this a lot of thought," I said.

"Some," John said, nodding. "You should probably know that I always try to live by my personal mantra." He smiled and paused for effect. "Either go big or go home."

"Yeah, I sort of figured that one out," I said, staring at him.

"But you wouldn't actually be on our staff, right?" Abby said.

"No, as much as I think I'd enjoy your company, I can't think of anything worse than sitting in an office all day. I'd be a contract consultant and set my own hours. And I have to warn you up front, I keep some very strange hours."

"We're going to need to discuss this," Abby said, setting her mug down on the counter.

"Absolutely," John said. "Take all the time you need." He beamed at all of us, then clapped his hands once. "Now, how about we go take some pictures and see if we can turn these gorgeous dogs into stars?"

He gestured at his assistant, and they strolled toward the far end of the loft. I watched them go, then turned to Thomas.

"How well do you know this guy?" I said.

"Really well," he said. "We went to high school together for a couple years. Then John took the equivalency exam and graduated early."

"To go to college?" I said.

"No, to do this," Thomas said, spreading his arms. "I'm going to go give them a hand getting ready."

He wandered off, and I sipped my coffee, deep in thought.

"He's an impressive young man," Abby said.

"Yes. And incredibly annoying," Josie said. "Smug central."

"He's really smart," Chef Claire said, then nodded to the far end of the loft where John was rolling around on the floor with all six dogs. "And he's a dog lover."

"Yeah, you can't fake that," Josie said, watching the action. "So, what do you guys think?"

"The worst thing that could happen is that we only get a free marketing campaign out of it," I said. "What do you think Abby? You'd be the one dealing with him most of the time."

"If he can drive the numbers anywhere close to what he says he can, I don't care how annoying he is. I'll figure out a way to deal with him."

"Okay, then I guess we'll give the kid a shot, right?" I said, glancing around.

"Shouldn't you check with your mother first?" Abby said. "She does own twenty percent of the company."

24

"Are you kidding?" I said, shaking my head. "My mother is gonna love this guy."

"I knew he reminded me of somebody," Josie said, laughing.

Chapter 3

I looked out the bank of windows that filled the back wall of the loft, then noticed a door next to the windows that led out to a large patio. Other industrial-style buildings that I assumed had also been converted into lofts were nearby but barely visible as the snow continued to fall. A pure white blanket dominated the landscape, and from inside, the winter scene was idyllic. But I was certain it would be miserable being out in it, especially since we'd arrived in town completely unprepared to deal with two feet of snow. I glanced over at John and his assistant, Melinda, who were making a few final changes and decided I had a few minutes before we were ready to start. I grabbed my phone, and Max answered on the second ring.

"Hey," he said. "I'm glad you called. Your phone has been off, and I was getting worried."

"We made it in," I said. "Barely. I can't believe how hard it's snowing. Where are you?"

"I decided to work from home today," Max said. "Are you guys at the shoot?"

"Yeah, we're about to get started," I said. "Have the plows made it to your street yet?"

"No, I'm on a side street that ends in a cul-de-sac," Max said. "It's a pretty low priority on the city's list. They probably won't make it to my street until sometime later on tonight. Where's the photographer's place?"

"He has a loft at the Wilkerson," I said. "Fifth floor with an amazing view of the city."

"Nice," Max said. "That's pretty close to my house."

"That's good because it's a total mess outside. But we'll figure out a way to get there," I said, glancing out again at the snow-covered streets.

"If worse comes to worse, you can always just walk. It can't be more than a couple of miles."

"Sure, sure," I said, frowning.

"Are you guys going to be hungry when you get here?"

"Rhetorical, right?"

"Yeah, I should know better by now," Max said, laughing. "I thought I'd make a stew. Or maybe a pot of chili."

"Perfect. Look, I gotta run. Can't wait to see you."

"Me too. Call me later when you get a chance."

"Will do."

I ended the call, turned the phone off, and tossed it on a nearby couch. John was chatting with Melinda and Abby. Apparently satisfied with their plan, they nodded in unison and John headed for a wall switch near the bank of windows. He stood quietly as he waited for a signal from Melinda that she was ready.

"You have an incredible view," I said to John.

"Yeah, I like it," he said, glancing over his shoulder out one of the windows. "It's great in the summer when I can open them to catch the breeze, and I love sitting out on the patio at night."

His assistant turned on two large lights that sat on either side of a rug that filled the area John would be using for the shoot. All the dogs snapped to attention and focused on the lights and reflector screens Melinda was adjusting.

"Okay, I think we're ready to go," John said, pressing the wall switch.

A black set of drapes slowly descended from the ceiling and soon covered the bank of windows. John stood in the middle of the rug and glanced around. Satisfied with the lighting, he nodded at his assistant.

"It looks great, Melinda. Okay, let's get this show on the road," he said, scanning the immediate area. "Where's that box of dog toys and props?"

"It's next to the couch," Melinda said. "Hang on, I'll grab it."

"I thought we'd start with some solo shots of each dog," John said, glancing around at all of us. "Then we'll work our way up to some group shots. We're going for fun, healthy, and happy." He smiled as he looked around at all the dogs. "With this group, that shouldn't be a problem. How about we start with the big guy? His name is Captain, right?"

"It is," Josie said. "But I need to warn you he hates wearing anything except his collar."

"Really?" Melinda cooed as she knelt down in front of the Newfie and unfurled a large woolen scarf. "You're such a good boy. What's the matter, Captain? You don't feel like wearing a scarf? It's cute and would look so good on you. They'd be calling you the Natty Newfie."

Captain snorted, scrambled to his feet, then crawled under a couch and disappeared from sight. Everyone laughed.

"He can be pretty stubborn about it," Josie said, shrugging.

Josie tried not to laugh as she watched John's assistant, Melinda, do her best to coax Captain out from underneath the couch. He finally poked his head out and glanced around then woofed his displeasure at Josie.

"You're such a baby," Josie said, kneeling down to rub his head.

"I guess we'll come back to him later," John said, shaking his head as he focused on Chloe. "How about you? You feel like getting your picture taken?"

Chloe headed straight for the rug and sat down and cocked her head at Melinda.

"I think she likes the idea," Melinda said, laughing.

"She loves to play dress up," I said.

"Yeah, we're still not sure who she gets that from," Josie deadpanned.

I made a face at her then focused on Chloe who was now wearing the scarf and holding one of the dog toys in her mouth.

"Oh, keep her right there," John said, taking several shots in rapid succession. "She's doing great. Okay, let's see how she looks wearing the fedora." He kept shooting dozens of pictures as Melinda removed the scarf and positioned the hat on Chloe's head. "Great. She's unbelievable. Now, scatter a bunch of the other toys around her and let's see how she does."

Chloe sat quietly as Melinda spread a dozen different toys on the rug near her. She dropped the toy she was holding and glanced at me.

"You think you can get her to try all the toys?" John said, not looking up from the viewfinder.

"Sure," I said, then focused on Chloe. "Go ahead, girl. Play with the toys."

Chloe selected one of the toys and held it in her mouth as Melinda approached and rearranged the other toys. We spent several minutes watching Chloe work her way through all the toys even as Melinda kept swapping out different scarves and hats. I swelled with pride and looked around at the others who were amazed by her performance. Finally, John lowered his camera and stood up.

"That is one smart dog," he said. "Did you teach her to do all that?"

"Just a little of it," I said, shrugging. "Most of it seems to come naturally to her."

"Spooky," John said, kneeling down to pet Chloe. "This is my kind of dog."

"Yeah, she's pretty special," I said.

"She is indeed," Josie said, then glanced down at Captain who was still staring out at the action from underneath the couch. "But you, you're such a disappointment," she said, laughing.

Captain woofed at Josie then went back to watching the photo shoot.

"Okay, let's see how the Goldens handle it," John said, glancing at Chef Claire. "Maybe we can get them to play tug of war with one of the toys."

Al and Dente trotted onto the rug and made a beeline for the same toy. Within seconds, they both had one end of it in their mouths and were growling playfully at each other.

"Yeah, I think we can probably make that happen," Chef Claire said, grinning at her Goldens.

John resumed shooting. Then he swapped out the Goldens with Abby's spaniels. Fifteen minutes later, he paused and glanced at Captain.

"Okay, Big Guy," he said to Captain. "Your turn."

Captain woofed at him and slid back further under the couch. Josie headed for the rug and returned with one of the toys. She placed it on the floor in front of the couch. Captain stared at it, then cocked his head at Josie.

"No, you're going to have to come out from underneath the couch if you want it," she said. "Come on, get your toy."

Captain snorted but gradually inched his way out and grabbed the toy.

"Good boy," Josie said, nodding. "Now, go play with it on the rug."

Captain trotted onto the rug and stretched out with the toy in his mouth. John and Melinda stared at each other.

"These guys are amazing," he said, snapping several shots of Captain.

"You want to try a hat or a scarf on him?" Melinda said.

"No, let's not push our luck," John said. "But let's see if we can get all of the other dogs next to him for a group shot." He glanced over at us. "Do you think we can make that happen? If not, I should be able to Photoshop them all in later."

"We can do that," I said, glancing at Josie and Chef Claire who both nodded. "Chloe, go say hi to Captain."

Chloe trotted over and sat down behind Captain then draped her head over his neck. Captain continued to focus on his toy.

"Let's go, guys," Chef Claire said as she headed for the rug. Both Goldens followed her, and they sat down behind Captain. "Good dogs. Stay." Chef Claire returned to where we were standing a few feet away.

"You guys set the bar pretty high," Abby said, laughing.

"See if you can get the Springers to lay down in front of the Newfie," John said, raising his camera.

"That I can do," Abby said. "C'mon, guys."

Moments later, all six dogs were holding dog toys in their mouths as they lounged together on the rug. Several other toys, all part of the new Wags' collection, were scattered around the rug. John shot continuously for the next few minutes then lowered the camera and stood up. The dogs stayed right where they were.

"Wow, that was way too easy," he said. "These are going to look fantastic."

"Look at them," I said, shaking my head in amazement. "It's like they're all smiling."

"It is," Josie said. "They're all very happy."

"Content," Chef Claire said. "Like they don't have a care in the world."

"That's probably because they don't," Josie said.

"That's it," John said, nodding his head as he continued to study the dogs.

"What?" I said, glancing over at him.

"The tagline for the company," he said. "I've been trying to come up with the right one." He continued to nod his head. "It's perfect."

We all looked at him and waited.

"Wags: The Happiest Dogs On Earth."

"Oh, that's good," Abby said.

John beamed as he glanced back and forth at us.

"I'm going to assume that we have a deal," he said.

Abby looked over at us and waited for us to respond. I glanced at Josie and Chef Claire who nodded immediately. I smiled at our CEO and gave her two thumbs up. Abby smiled back then turned to John.

"We got a deal."

Chapter 4

John and Melinda huddled for a few moments, then outlined their next steps to us. And after everyone had agreed to reconnect tomorrow, weather permitting, to review the mockups they would be working on tonight, we loaded the dogs into the SUV and headed for the parking garage exit. I was pleased to see that one of the building maintenance staff was just finishing snow blowing the exit ramp that led out to the street. At the bottom of the ramp, I made a right onto the freshly-plowed street and merged into light traffic.

"This might not be so bad," I said, glancing over at Josie in the passenger seat.

"Don't speak too soon," she said. "It's bad luck to tempt fate."

"I doubt if the hand of fate is interested in whether or not the city streets are plowed," I said, frowning at her.

"Hey, don't say I didn't warn you," she said, then glanced out the window at the blanket of white that dominated the city. "I can't wait to see what they come up with."

"Me too," I said, glancing down to review the directions Max had given me. I slowed to confirm the name of the street then put my turn signal on. "That was quick."

I made a left onto a street that had been plowed earlier. But several inches of new snow had already accumulated since then, and I slowed to a crawl to work my way around a couple of cars parked on the side of the street and half-buried by what the plow had shoved over them. I noticed the street sign that matched Max's address and was about to make the right turn when I pumped the brakes. I came to a stop and stared at the five-foot-high snowbank that was blocking access to Max's street.

"Uh-oh," I said, staring at the wall of snow the plows had left behind. "It looks like a couple of the plows decided to build a snow fort."

"I told you not to talk about it," Josie said, shaking her head at the scene right outside the car. "Now what do we do?"

"What's the problem?" Chef Claire said, leaning forward from the back seat.

"The plows somehow managed to leave a wall of snow blocking access to Max's street," I said. "I suppose we could just try to drive through it."

"Bad idea," Josie said. "The last thing we want is to get stuck in a snowbank. Not to mention what it might do your car."

"Yeah, you're right," I said, nodding. "Let me give Max a call and see what he has to say." I grabbed my bag and searched for my phone. Moments later, I looked over at Josie. "I can't find my phone."

"Where did you leave it?" Josie said.

"I thought I put it back in my bag," I said, digging through it again. "But it's not here. I must have left it in the loft."

"Not a problem," Josie said. "You can pick it up tomorrow. I'll call Max. What's his number?"

I frowned as I tried to remember it. Eventually, I glanced over at her and shook my head.

"I don't know it," I said. "Since it's stored on my phone, I never bothered to memorize it."

"Okay," Josie said, shrugging. "I'll just call information."

Josie got Max's number then called.

"Busy signal," she said, handing me the phone. "But it just went to voicemail."

I took the phone from her and left a message for Max explaining what had happened and where we were. I ended the call and handed her phone back.

"I guess we just wait here, right?" Josie said, yawning.

"Why don't we just go back to the loft and get my phone now?" I said. "It would only take a few minutes."

"Why not?" Josie said, shrugging as she made another call.

"Who are you calling?" I said, turning the car around.

"You," she said, holding her phone to her ear.

"Hello, this is Suzy," I said, grinning at her.

"Funny," Josie said, then ended the call. "It went straight to voicemail. Your phone must be off."

"Thomas would have Naylor's cell number, right?" I said, making a right.

"Good thinking," Josie said, making the call. "Hey, Thomas. It's Josie. Good, thanks. Yeah, today's shoot was a lot of fun. Look, Suzy thinks she left her phone at John's place and wants to give him a call. Yeah, I need his number." Josie jotted the number down. "Thanks. You sound out of breath. You're at the gym? In this weather? Okay, have fun with that. We'll see you tomorrow." She ended the call, then entered John's number. "Who the heck would go to the gym in the middle of a snowstorm?"

"You're asking me?" I said, glancing over as I put my turn signal on.

"Yeah, I forgot who I was talking to," she said, the phone to her ear. "Naylor's phone must be turned off." She lowered the phone and stared out the window. "Did you get a number from his assistant?"

"Melinda? No," I said. "It's okay. We're almost there. I'll just pull into the parking garage and run up and get it."

I spotted John's building and slowed down then drove up the ramp that led to guest parking. I hopped out and glanced into the back where the dogs were beginning to stir.

"No, Chloe. Stay." I glanced at Josie and Chef Claire. "I'll be right back," I said, closing the door and heading for the elevator that led to the lobby.

I checked in with security then headed for the elevators. One of the doors opened immediately, and I punched the five and leaned against the back of the elevator as the door closed and began its ascent. The door opened, and I headed down the hall doing my best lumber. I was sure it wasn't anything like the workout Thomas must be going through at the gym, but it certainly got my heart pumping.

I decided to count it.

I came to a stop outside the door and took a second to catch my breath. I knocked on the door and was surprised when the door slid open a few inches. My neurons flared as I gently pushed the door and poked my head inside.

"John?"

I waited for a response then called out again. Hearing nothing, I stepped inside and closed the door behind me. I took small steps as I moved forward scanning the loft, my eyes slowly moving left to right then back the other way. I paused near the kitchen area and scanned the counter for my phone. I listened closely for sounds that might indicate the presence of someone else. Hearing nothing, I continued toward the back of the loft where we'd done the photo shoot. I glanced around and noticed that the lights and the rug we'd used had been removed and that the drapes had been raised. I glanced out the windows at the snow that continued to fall.

"John? Hello. Is anybody here?"

I looked around for signs of a wall phone, but the closest I came was an intercom on a wall near the kitchen. I noticed an identical intercom near the front door. Thinking that perhaps John had found my phone and had put it in his office for safekeeping, I walked toward the office area that, like the bedroom, was cordoned off from the rest of the loft by an elaborate set of Japanese screens. There was nothing on the glass desktop, and it was sparkling clean. I sat down in the chair behind the desk and began opening various drawers. After finding all four empty, I sat back in the chair and felt the hairs on the back of my neck begin to tingle as a sense of dread descended over me. A busy man like Naylor certainly must have had at least some paper files or documents in his office, but there was nothing. I also noticed the lack of camera equipment and the laptop he'd used earlier during the shoot.

I stood up to continue my search and headed for the bedroom. I made my way into the large space and noticed John's assistant, Melinda, fully clothed and sound asleep on the large bed that dominated the room. I was about to wake her up, then I jumped back. I stared down at her and recognized the vacant stare immediately.

"Oh, no," I whispered as I headed for the bed. I leaned over for a closer look, then stood up and shook my head as tears welled in my eyes. I started to reach for her wrist to check for a pulse, then stopped when I noticed a white powder on the pillow underneath her head. I took a step back and started to sob. A look of surprise was fixed on the young woman's face, and I backed out of the bedroom, my eyes darting back and forth as the thought that whoever had killed the young woman might still be in the loft popped into my head. I made my way to the intercom near the kitchen, grabbed a knife from its butcher block holder and stood with my back to the wall glancing around the loft. I pressed the intercom button.

"Hello?" I said. "Is anybody there?"

"This is security," a man said.

"Oh, it's you," I said, relaxing a bit when I heard the familiar voice.

"I'm sorry," the confused voice said.

"I just checked in with you a few minutes ago," I said.

"Sure, I remember," the security guard said. "You were heading back up to John Naylor's place on five. And judging by what I see on my system, you're still there. How can I help you?"

"There's…a problem up here," I stammered.

"I see," he said, suddenly on edge. "What sort of problem?"

"I think you should get up here right away," I said. "I'm pretty sure there's been an intruder."

"And why do you think that?"

"Mainly because of the dead woman in the bedroom," I said as a torrent of tears began to stream down my cheeks.

"Stay right there," he snapped. "And don't touch anything."

I remained rigid with my back against the wall and continued to scan the loft. A few minutes later, I heard a knock on the door. I headed to the door and reached for the handle.

"Who is it?" I said, before opening the door.

"It's me. Security."

Still holding the knife, I slowly opened the door, and the security guard stepped inside, saw the terror in my eyes, and held his hands up.

"It's okay, I'm here," he said, motioning for me to put the knife down. "Are you hurt?"

"No," I said, setting the knife down on the floor.

"You said there was a woman in the bedroom," he said, leaning down to pick up the knife.

"Yes, there is," I said.

"Okay, just stay here while I take a look," he said, heading toward the back of the loft.

"I think I'll come with you if it's all right with you," I said, following him.

"I suppose that would be okay," he said, glancing back over his shoulder. "Just don't touch anything."

"Aren't you going to pull your gun?"

"Most security guards in Canada aren't armed," he said, approaching the bedroom.

"They aren't?" I said, frowning.

"No."

"Why not?"

"We Canadians have found that having fewer people carrying guns cuts way down on the number of people getting shot," he said, then stopped in his tracks. "The woman in the bedroom wasn't shot, was she?"

"No, she wasn't," I said, shaking my head. "I don't know how she was killed, but I did see powder on one of the pillows."

"You're sure she's dead?"

"Yes. I'm sure."

The security guard stepped inside the bedroom, exhaled loudly as he shook his head, and examined the body without touching it. He nodded for me to follow him, and he walked back into the main area of the loft and grabbed his phone from his pocket. He placed a call, spoke briefly to the person on the other end of the line, then hung up and made a second call. This one lasted longer and judging from his end of the conversation it was apparent he was speaking with the police. I sat down in a chair and wiped my eyes with a handful of tissues. The security guard finished the call, put his phone away, and sat down in a chair facing me.

"The police are on their way," he said, shaking his head. "That poor girl."

"You knew her?"

"Sure. Enough to say hi and chat. She was around all the time since she worked for Mr. Naylor."

My neurons fired.

"Can I borrow your phone? I need to make a call."

"Sure," he said, handing it to me.

I concentrated hard trying to remember Josie's number then dialed it. She answered on the first ring.

"This is Josie."

43

"Hey, it's me," I said.

"What's keeping you?" she said. "Can't find your phone?"

"No, I didn't find it," I said, exhaling audibly. "But there's a problem up here."

"What sort of problem?"

"Melinda."

"Naylor's assistant? What's the matter with her?"

"She's dead."

I waited out a long silence.

"Okay," Josie said. "I'm going to go out on a limb and assume you didn't kill her."

"No, but I'm the one who found her body," I said, rubbing my forehead. "And that means I'm probably going to be tied up here for at least a couple of hours."

I glanced at the security guard who nodded his head in agreement.

"So, you guys might as well head back to Max's place. I'll either have the police drop me off when they're done with me, or I'll take a cab."

"Max just called," Josie said. "He said that he and a neighbor are going to take their snow blowers out and clear the snowbank that's blocking the street."

"Okay," I said. "Just head back to his place and let the dogs do their business. They must be busting by now. I'll give you a call later on as soon as I know anything."

"Got it," she said. "You need anything before we take off?"

"No, I'm good," I said. "But drive careful. And tell Max I'm sorry the weekend is getting off to such a lousy start."

"I'm sure he'll forgive you," Josie said.

"When are we going to Cayman?" I said, forcing a small laugh.

"Not soon enough."

"Oh, you might want to try calling Naylor's phone again," I said, my neurons slowly beginning to kick into overdrive.

"I called a few minutes ago," Josie said. "His phone is still off."

"Okay," I said, nodding. "If you get a chance, keep trying to get in touch with him. He needs to know what happened here. And you might want to see if you can get hold of Thomas. Maybe he knows where John is."

"Will do. Get out of there as soon as you can."

"I'll do my best," I said.

"Oh, Suzy. Just one more thing."

"Yeah?"

"Try to keep your Snoopmeter in neutral," Josie said, her voice rising a notch to emphasize her point.

"Sure, sure."

Chapter 5

While we waited for the police to arrive, the security guard and I chatted. I learned that his name was Gilbert, liked to be called Gil, was a vegan who was working his way through school, and had hopes of becoming a physical education teacher or fitness instructor with yoga as the central tenet. As much as I admired his focus and dedication to his life goals, as you might imagine, most of our chitchat was short and perfunctory.

In a concerted effort to keep my mind off the dead body in the bedroom, I tried to pay close attention to what Gil was telling me. But after patiently listening to him recite his ten favorite ways to prepare Brussel Sprouts, and discuss the two hours he did six days a week on his stationary bike, my neurons were screaming for relief. And by the time he covered in great detail how much he enjoyed snacking on raw tempeh and boiled veggie dogs while he was on his bike, I was squirming in my chair and almost threw up in my mouth. I forced my neurons to chase away all thoughts about his dietary choices and focused on the insane yet far less troubling notion of a daily, two-hour bike ride that never left the living room.

But Gil did turn about to be a dog lover, and that fact broke several awkward silences and saved the day. We were deep into a debate about the best breed of water dogs when we heard a loud knock on the door. He hopped to his feet and headed for the door. I glanced at the two detectives heading my way and almost fell out of my chair.

"I don't believe it," I said, standing up and smiling as I glanced back and forth at them.

"Suzy Chandler," Detective Shirley Billet said, extending her hand. "What on earth are you doing here?"

"Hi, Shirley," I said, shaking her hand. I extended my hand to the other detective. "Hi, Bill."

"Hello, Suzy," Detective Bill Franklin said, shaking his head in disbelief as he returned the handshake. "This oughta be good."

"Questions?" I said, glancing back and forth at them.

"About a dozen come straight to mind," Shirley said, looking at her partner.

I'd met the two detectives the last time we'd been in Ottawa. Josie and I had been speaking at a conference where the CEO of Middleton Enterprises, the largest pet store franchise in North America and now Wags' exclusive retail distributor, had been killed. Much to their initial dismay, I had inserted myself into the investigation and later played a major role in solving the murder. I'd also learned that Bill was a widower who was secretly involved with Shirley, and they had finally decided to go public. Judging by the rock on her left hand, they'd recently decided to take the relationship to the next level. Shirley noticed the look I was giving her engagement ring, and she held her hand out so I could get a better look.

"Impressive," I said, nodding. "You moonlighting as a jewelry thief, Detective?"

"Funny," Bill said.

"Congratulations," I said, beaming at them. "I'm very happy for you." I looked at Shirley. "Have you guys set a date yet?"

"We're looking at June," Shirley said.

"Nice," I said, nodding. "Are you having the wedding outside?"

"Yeah, we're leaning that way," Shirley said. "But I'm worried about bad weather."

"Give me a call," I said. "My mother works with an amazing tent guy. She uses him all the time."

"Thanks," Shirley said. "I'll do that."

"What about the honeymoon? Where are you guys going?"

"We're still undecided," Shirley said, putting her hands on her hips. "There are just so many choices."

"Yeah, I know," I said, nodding. "But as long as you're there together, it shouldn't matter where you decide to go, right?"

"I guess."

Bill cleared his throat and Shirley and I glanced at him, red-faced.

"Sorry," Shirley said, then transitioned back into detective. She looked at the security guard. "Why don't you take us to the body?"

"Sure, follow me," Gil said, heading toward the bedroom area.

"I think I'll wait here," I said, sitting back down.

I sat quietly until they returned about fifteen minutes later. The security guard said his goodbyes then left. The two detectives sat down on a couch across from me, and both pulled out a pen and notepad and stared at me.

"You want to play twenty questions or would you like me to just start talking?" I said, glancing back and forth at them.

"Let's start with you talking," Bill said. "Then we'll do the twenty-question thing."

"Good call," I said. "I'm in town with my other business partners for some meetings regarding our new dog toy business. You remember the dog toys that the murderer's sister created?"

"We do," Bill said.

"Well, we bought the company from her before she went to jail, and we're getting ready to launch."

"I see," Bill said, scribbling a note. "Congratulations."

"Thanks," I said, then provided a quick summary of the day. When I finished, I sat back and waited for the questions to begin.

"Why did you decide to use John Naylor as your photographer?" Shirley said.

"He's a friend of our head of logistics. Thomas Steel," I said. "Do you remember the woman who organized the conference where Middleton was killed?"

"Yes, I do," Shirley said. "Marjorie, right?"

"You've got a good memory," I said. "Thomas is her son."

"Okay," Shirley said. "But today was the first time you'd met Naylor and the victim, right?"

"Yes."

"And you're positive that the victim, Melinda, was still in the loft when you left this afternoon?" Bill said.

"Definitely," I said, nodding. "She was the one who walked us to the door."

"Okay," Shirley said. "How long was it from the time you left this afternoon until you came back to the loft?"

"Let me think," I said, my neurons flaring. "We left just before three. And we waited forever for the elevator. It probably took us five minutes to get back to the car, another five to get all the dogs in and settled down. Then the drive to my boyfriend's place took about ten minutes. Access to his street was blocked by a snowbank the plows had left behind, so we turned around and came back here. I thought I'd left my phone here. I parked in the garage downstairs and headed straight back up to the loft. It couldn't have been more than forty-five minutes. Maybe a bit less."

"That's not a lot of time," Bill said, frowning.

"Well, the plows had been out, so the streets were pretty clear," I said, shrugging.

"I was referring to the amount of time that elapsed before she was killed," Bill said.

"Oh. Sorry," I said, embarrassed. "No, I guess it's not a lot of time."

"Did you pick up on anything between the woman and Naylor?" Shirley said.

"Not really," I said, shaking my head. "Apart from the fact that it was pretty clear they had a good working relationship."

"How so?" she said, pen poised.

"They were very efficient," I said. "It was like they'd developed a sort of shorthand working together." I glanced back and forth at them. "Sort of like the one you guys have."

The detectives both nodded and jotted down notes.

"Any indication that they had more than a working relationship?" Bill said.

"You mean, sort of like the one you guys have?" I said, grinning.

"How about you try to keep a lid on the annoyance factor?" Bill said. "You were doing so well."

"I thought it was funny," I said, shrugging.

"Me too," Shirley said, laughing. Then she refocused. "You haven't seen Naylor since you left this afternoon?"

"No, we tried calling him a couple of times after I realized I'd forgotten my phone," I said. "But all the calls went straight to voicemail."

"Have you spoken to anyone?" Shirley said.

"We managed to get hold of Thomas," I said. "He was at the gym."

"Do you have his address?" Bill said.

"No, but I can definitely get that for you," I said. "What do you think was the cause of death? I took a quick look when I discovered the body, but it didn't look like she had any injuries."

"She doesn't," Shirley said, glancing at Bill who shrugged as if to say go ahead. "It looks like there's some sort of powder on the pillows."

"Yeah, I saw that," I said, my neurons firing as I flashed back to what I'd seen in the bedroom earlier. "What do you think it is?"

"We're not sure yet," Shirley said.

"But not a drug, right?" I said, frowning.

"Probably more like a poison," Bill said.

"Somebody sprinkled poison powder on the pillows?" I said.

"That's our best guess at the moment," Shirley said.

"But if that's the case, wouldn't that mean that Naylor was the intended victim?"

"That's also our best guess at the moment," Bill said. "And given Naylor's reputation, it's a pretty good assumption."

"Because of the tabloid photos he takes, right?" I said.

"I thought you said you just met the guy," Bill said, raising an eyebrow at me. "How the heck would you know that?"

"Really, Bill?" I said, scowling at him. "After all we've been through, you're going to start suspecting me?"

"I'm not suspecting you," he snapped. "I'm just wondering how you knew that."

"The security guard was talking to one of my business partners earlier," I said, shrugging. "He mentioned a few things about the Naylor's lifestyle."

"I think we might need to have another chat with him," Bill said, scribbling another note.

"It couldn't hurt," Shirley said, also writing in her notepad. "And as a security guard, he might have a way to access all the residences."

"I'm sure he would," Bill said, nodding. "What else did the security guard have to say?"

"Let's see," I said, pressing my stomach to stop the hunger pangs that were beginning to make themselves heard. "He said that John does photoshoots with a lot of different models, loves to make money, and that he works all the time."

"Did he say anything about blackmail?" Bill said.

"What?" I said, staring at him. "Blackmail?"

"Rumor has it that Naylor isn't above trying to extort money from some of the people he manages to catch in compromising positions," Bill said.

"No, that is something I had not heard," I said, frowning. "Who has he blackmailed?"

"Like I said, at the moment, they're just rumors," he said, glancing around the loft. "And that's why we need to get our hands on his cameras and computers. The photos and videos he has stored on them should tell us a lot about who he might be going after."

"And maybe point us in the right direction about who might have been trying to kill him," Shirley said.

"Good luck with that," I said, glancing out the windows at the storm.

"Good luck with what?" Bill said, staring at me.

I felt my face flush red, and I took a few deep breaths before continuing.

"His office is empty," I said eventually.

"You searched the guy's office?" Bill said.

"Well, searched is such a strong term, Detective," I said, giving him a weak grin.

"Why on earth would you do that?" Shirley said.

"I was looking for my phone."

"I see," Bill said. "Had you spent any time in his office when you were here earlier?"

"No," I whispered.

"But you still thought it was okay to search the guy's office?" Bill said.

"Hey, it's always in the last place where you'd expect to find it, right?" I said, going for casual.

Shirley stifled a laugh and shook her head at me.

"All his cameras and equipment are gone?" Bill said, annoyed.

"Yeah. And his desk drawers are all empty."

"Okay," Bill said, nodding. "I think we might be getting close to a motive."

"I think we should start with the building management and get a list of all the security personnel and other office staff who might have access," Shirley said.

"Don't forget housekeeping," I said.

"Does this place even have a housekeeping staff?" Bill said.

"Take a look around," I said, flashing back to something I'd noticed in the bedroom. "Naylor is a twenty-three-year-old who works non-stop. And he doesn't seem to be the type who'd be willing to spend the amount of time required to keep the place looking like this."

"It is immaculate," Shirley said, glancing around the loft.

"Yeah, that's a good point. I remember what I was like at twenty-three when it came to cleaning up," Bill said, nodding as he took a long look at his surroundings.

"That's probably because when it comes to cleaning up after yourself, you're *still* in your twenties," Shirley said, glaring at him.

"Don't start," Bill said, returning her stare. "I said I'd try to do better."

"That was three months ago," she said.

"I've been busy."

"And I haven't?"

"Can we do this later?" Bill snapped.

"I'd rather you do the dishes," Shirley said with a shrug. "But I'll take what I can get." She nodded to herself, apparently satisfied with how the conversation had gone, then focused on me. "I think you might be right. Keeping the place looking like this would take a lot of work."

"And I seriously doubt if a twenty-three-year-old would spend that much time making his bed the way that one in there is. That's a hotel-quality job."

"Interesting," Shirley said. "If the building doesn't have a housekeeping staff, Naylor probably has someone come in."

"Someone with access to the loft," I said.

All three of us glanced up when he heard the door open. John Naylor entered carrying a large bundle of dry cleaning and two plastic bags. I immediately picked up a whiff of Chinese food and felt my stomach gurgle. Naylor set the food down on a table near the door and removed his coat without noticing our presence.

"I hope you're hungry, Melinda," he called out. "I got enough food to feed a small army. But I figured since we'll be working all night, we might want a snack later on. Oh, the dry cleaner said your black sweater won't be ready for a few-" He stopped short when he finally noticed us and frowned. "Suzy? What are you doing here?"

"Uh, I forgot my phone and stopped by to pick it up."

"Yeah, I saw it earlier on the couch near the windows," he said, walking toward us. "I was going to try to get in touch with you later and let you know I had it. But how the heck did you get in?" He stopped in front of us and glanced back and forth at the two cops. "Hi, I'm John Naylor. Are you friends of Suzy?"

"We are," Shirley said. "But that's not why we're here, Mr. Naylor."

"Mr. Naylor," the photographer said, laughing. "That sounds official."

"I'm Detective Franklin," Bill said. "And this is Detective Billet."

"Okay," John said, confused. He focused on me. "Why are the cops here? Did someone break in?"

"I'm afraid we have some bad news for you, Mr. Naylor," Bill said.

"I imagine you rarely show up to deliver good news," John said.

"Fair point," Bill said, nodding. "It's about your assistant Melinda."

"What about her?"

The detectives looked at each other, then Shirley gave her partner a small nod for him to proceed.

"She's dead," Bill said softly.

"What?"

"It appears she's been murdered," Shirley said. "I'm so sorry, Mr. Naylor."

"That's ridiculous," John said, glancing around at us, wide-eyed. "Melinda's the sweetest person I know. No one would want to kill her."

"If that's the case, and we think you might be right," Bill said. "That means there's only one other logical conclusion we can come to, Mr. Naylor."

Naylor stood still in the middle of the loft looking off into the distance. Then he stared at Bill.

"Somebody was trying to kill me."

He slowly made his way to the couch and plopped down. He leaned forward with his elbows on his knees and stared down at the floor.

"Do you have any idea who might want to kill you, Mr. Naylor?" Bill said.

"Well, I know several people I've annoyed in the past," John said, not looking up. "But I seriously doubt if I've given any of them enough of a reason to kill me." Then he glanced toward the bedroom. "Would it be okay for me to take a look at Melinda?"

"That's probably not a good idea," Bill said.

"I'd like to see her," John said. "And say goodbye."

"They'll be plenty of time for that later, Mr. Naylor," Bill said. "I'm sorry, but at the moment, it's still a crime scene."

"All right," John said, exhaling loudly. "I'm sorry, Suzy. I'm afraid we're going to have to rearrange our schedule."

"That's the least of our worries, John."

"Maybe I can get started in a couple of days after things settle down," he said.

"That might be a problem, John."

"What are you talking about?"

"I was in your office earlier looking for my phone," I said. "And it looks like all your stuff is gone."

"What?" he said, jumping to his feet and headed straight for his office.

Bill started to follow him, then stopped and turned back to us.

"I need to keep an eye on him and make sure he doesn't go near the body," Bill said. "Suzy, you should probably get going. Just make sure Shirley knows how to get in touch with you."

"Okay," I said. "But there is one small problem."

"What's that?" Shirley said.

"I need a ride."

Chapter 6

I was sitting in the passenger seat of the cop car, which was actually a large SUV equipped with four-wheel drive. Shirley had both hands on the wheel and was driving slowly on the snow-covered streets deep in thought. I unzipped my jacket to deal with the heater that had turned the inside of the car into a dry sauna, and the incongruity of me sweating profusely while a wind-whipped snowstorm continued unabated outside was a not so gentle reminder of the approaching winter wonderland residents would be dealing with for the next several months.

"Too hot?" Shirley said, glancing over at me.

"Maybe a little," I said, pulling the front of my wool sweater away from my skin.

"Sorry," she said, turning the heat down. "This is the way Bill likes it, and I guess I've finally gotten used to it."

"What is he? Part furnace?" I said, wiping my brow with a sleeve.

"He does tend to blow hot air from time to time," Shirley said, laughing.

"He's a good guy," I said, nodding. "And congrats again on the wedding."

"Thanks. So, tell me about this new guy you're seeing."

"Max? He's great," I said, smiling. "We've been dating a couple of months. He's a disaster relief consultant."

Shirley flinched then glanced over at me.

"You're dating Max Jenkins?"

"Yeah. Do you know Max?"

"Only by reputation," Shirley said. "He's kind of a folk hero around here."

"Really?" I said, frowning.

"A guy who spends his own money to go into disaster areas and help people?" Shirley said. "What would you call him?"

"No, I get all that," I said. "I just wasn't aware that a lot of people knew what he does. He doesn't like to talk about it."

"I don't think many people did know about him," Shirley said. "Until those tabloid photos were published."

My stomach sunk.

"Tabloid photos?"

"Yeah, about a year ago there were some shots of him coming out the back door of a club with a very drunk woman. He was holding her up with one hand and trying to fend off a photographer with the other."

"Who was the woman?"

"Jennifer Bells," Shirley said, glancing over, apparently expecting me to know who she was talking about.

I shook my head and shrugged.

"She was the Foreign Affairs Minister at the time," Shirley said. "Her tenure ended shortly after that incident."

"Max was dating her?" I said, frowning.

"That was the original assumption when the photos were first published. And they weren't very flattering to the Minister. One of them was snapped when they were trying to get her in the car, and she came to momentarily, threw a punch at the photographer then threw up on him," she said.

"Yuk," I said. "And the photos made all the papers?"

"They certainly did. Along with pretty much every celebrity website. I'm surprised you didn't see them."

"It actually does sound vaguely familiar," I said. "But I wouldn't have made the connection back then."

"No, of course not. But when the real story finally came out, we learned that our former Foreign Affairs Minister is Max's aunt. His mother's sister. Apparently, Max's mom called him and asked him to go to the club to get her out of there."

"He's never mentioned it," I said.

"Like you said, he's pretty private. Anyway, what he does for a living came out in the story, and ever since then, some of the journalists have taken an interest in keeping an eye on him. Especially when he heads off on a new adventure. The Canadian press has started calling him Supermax. You know, a play on Superman."

"Got it," I said, nodding. "What happened to his aunt?"

"Well, they were eventually able to confirm that somebody had slipped something into her drink at the club. But by then it was too late. She had already resigned. I think she still lives around here somewhere," Shirley said, glancing over and giving me a small smile. "Take a guess who was spotted talking with her at the bar earlier in the evening."

I stared out at the swirling snow deep in thought. Then my neurons flared and eventually landed.

"John Naylor."

"You're good," Shirley said. "There was no proof, but most people believe he was the one who spiked her drink and that he had someone waiting outside the club with a camera."

"That's despicable," I said.

"Naylor denies it to this day. But what else would you expect him to do, right?"

"This is too weird," I said, catching a glimpse of the street sign. "This is it. Make a right."

Shirley slowly made the turn onto Max's street. The snowbank blocking access had been cleared, but the street itself still hadn't been plowed.

"Are you going to be able to drive through this?" I said.

"Sure," Shirley said, slowing down. "This is nothing. I grew up in this crap."

"Did they ever identify the photographer who was waiting outside the club?" I said.

"They did not," Shirley said. "It was confirmed it was a guy, but that's about it. Everybody on the scene was more concerned about getting Jennifer out of there. And the photographer took off before they could get their hands on him or his camera."

"And now somebody is trying to kill Naylor," I said, my neurons firing on all cylinders.

"I doubt if the two are connected," Shirley said, shaking her head. "But it does show you the sort of thing Naylor likes to get involved with."

"But why would he do stuff like that?" I said, shaking my head. "He's so talented. And obviously very smart."

"Who knows what motivates people like him? And I've met a lot of very smart and talented crooks."

I caught a glimpse of my SUV parked in a driveway ahead on our right.

"That's the house," I said, pointing.

"Nice neighborhood," Shirley said, slowing down.

"You want to come in and meet everyone?"

"Normally, I would," Shirley said, pulling into the driveway behind my vehicle. "But I need to get back and help Bill out. We've got a long night ahead of us. You got a number where we can reach you in case we find your phone?"

I dug through my purse, located a business card, then scribbled Josie's cell number on the back. I handed it over and zipped my coat up.

"Thanks for the ride," I said, opening the door.

"No problem," Shirley said. "I'm sure we'll be chatting."

"Yeah, you can count on that."

Chapter 7

I waved goodbye to Shirley as she drove off then headed for the sidewalk that led to the front door. Max had been busy. Not only had he removed the snowbank blocking the entrance to the street, but he'd also used the snowblower to clear his driveway and sidewalk along with those of his neighbors on either side of his house. I climbed the front steps and rang the bell. Max, along with four very excited dogs, greeted me at the door. He pulled me in for a kiss and a long hug, then I knelt down to say hello to Chloe and the rest of our tribe.

"You made it," Max said.

"I'm sorry I'm so late," I said, standing up to give him another kiss. "But what can you do, huh?"

"Try spending less time around dead people?"

"Yeah, I really need to start working on that," I said, handing him my coat and following him into a large living room.

I spotted Josie and Chef Claire in their sweats sitting in front of the roaring fireplace that dominated the room. They were drinking wine and nibbling from a nosh plate that was on a small table between their chairs.

"Hey, you're alive," Josie said, grabbing a glass and holding it as Chef Claire poured. She handed me my wine, and I clinked glasses with both of them. "What's the update?"

"The cops think whoever killed her used some sort of poison," I said, sitting down on a couch and immediately making room for Chloe who was looking for more attention. "Yes, I missed you, too." I rubbed her head then she rolled over onto her back almost spilling my wine.

"Do they have an idea why anyone would want to poison her?" Chef Claire said. "She seemed like a sweetheart."

"They think Naylor was the intended target," I said, taking a sip.

Max slid onto the couch next to me and lifted his arms to give Chloe room to slide over. Soon, she had somehow managed to drape herself across a portion of both our laps. Max gently stroked her back legs, and Chloe's tail thumped against the cushion.

"We've spent the afternoon bonding," Max said. "So, somebody is trying to kill John Naylor."

"That's what it looks like," I said, draping an arm over his shoulder. "What's your take?"

"My take?" Max said, glancing at me. "I guess my take is to wonder why it's taken so long. He's done some pretty despicable things."

"Yes, so I've heard," I said, giving him a coy smile. "Supermax."

"Please don't call me that," Max said, frowning. "Who have you been talking to?"

"The cop who drove me home told me the story about your aunt at the club," I said.

"I guess that story is never going to go away," Max said softly. "That was a bad night."

"What is she doing these days?"

"Aunt Jennifer is writing a book about her partying days and what it did to her career," Max said. "Then she eventually wants to see if it's possible to make a comeback."

"And Naylor was definitely the guy behind what happened at the club?"

"That's the prevailing theory," Max said, nodding. "But Naylor has always been adamant that he wasn't involved. He maintains that he was merely trying to talk Aunt Jennifer into going home with him."

"Do you believe him?"

"Given all the other stuff he's pulled, probably not. Do the cops have any idea about who might be going after him?"

"No, not yet. They were hoping to identify some potential suspects by going through his camera and computer," I said, taking a sip. "But Naylor's loft was cleaned out."

"Does that mean they also got all the photos from our shoot?" Josie said.

"Yeah, apparently, they got everything," I said. "And since we're not going to be able to review the mockups with Naylor that means most of our day tomorrow just got freed up."

"We're going to have to do the photo shoot again?" Josie said, frowning.

"It looks like we might have to," I said.

"You want to rent some skis and go cross-country tomorrow?" Chef Claire said, glancing around the room.

"That sounds like fun," Max said, leaning forward, obviously interested. "There's a nice trail that runs behind the house." He glanced at me. "What do you say?"

"You really haven't been paying attention, have you?" I said, laughing. "You guys go ahead. Abby and I have a meeting with Victor Rollins."

"What do you say, Josie?" Chef Claire said.

Josie stared at Chef Claire and took a moment to formulate a response.

"No, I should stay here and keep an eye on the dogs," Josie said. "Other than that, I'd love to go."

"We'll just bring the dogs with us," Max said.

"What a great idea," Chef Claire said, grinning at Josie.

"You're not helping, Max," Josie said.

"Then it's settled," Max said, getting to his feet. Then he got an idea and glanced at me. "Maybe we should just wait until you get back from your meeting. What time will you finish?"

"Oh, I'm sure the meeting is going to run long," I said, deflecting. "Very long."

Josie snorted.

"Shut it. But you guys have fun."

"Sounds great," Max said. "There's a place just down the road where you guys can rent skis. If you'll excuse me for a few moments, I need to check on dinner."

He gently slid Chloe off his lap and started to head toward the kitchen but stopped when Josie called after him.

"Hang on. What was the Supermax comment all about?" she said.

"Oh, that. It's nothing," he said, embarrassed.

"Don't be modest. That's the nickname the local press has given him," I said, beaming at Max. "As a tribute to all the great work he does. You know, like Superman."

"Let's not do this," Max said, shaking his head.

"Supermax," Josie said, grinning. "I like it. Is it a plane? Is it a bird?"

"No, it's Supermax," Chef Claire said, laughing. "Faster than a speeding bullet."

"And they were so nice to me when we first met," Max said, glancing over at me. "What happened?"

"I'm surprised it lasted as long as it did. Welcome to the family."

"I'd like one of those tee shirts with the giant S on it," Josie deadpanned. "Women's medium. Light blue if you have it."

"Yeah, I'll see what I can do," Max said, shaking his head. "I'll meet you in the dining room in five."

"You need a hand?" I said.

"Of course, he doesn't," Josie said. "He's *Supermax*."

69

"I think we should start seeing other people," Max said to me then headed to the kitchen still shaking his head.

"You guys are bad," I said, shaking my head. "Oh, I almost forget to call my mother. I told her I'd check in tonight. Can I borrow your phone?"

Josie tossed the phone to me, and I gave my mother a quick call. She was having dinner at home with her boyfriend, Paulie, and I spent a few minutes giving her an overview of the day's events. After telling me three times to keep my nose out of the police investigation, she hung up, and I handed Josie her phone back.

"Thanks. It looks like I'm going to have to get a new phone," I said. "That ought to be a whole lot of fun."

"You don't keep any personal information or financial stuff on it, do you?" Chef Claire said, getting up out of her chair.

"No," I said, shaking my head. "I don't think there's much there apart from the basic information I had to put in when I got the phone."

"Good," Chef Claire said, nodding. "Because that could be a nightmare."

"Can the cops track a phone's location even if it's turned off?" I said as my neurons flared briefly.

"I think it depends," Chef Claire said. "There are definitely some phones you can do that with, but I think there are some settings that have to be turned on. Do you remember how your phone is set up?"

"I don't have a clue," I said, heading for the dining room. "I have a hard enough time just getting to voicemail."

"I'm sure the cops will be running various traces," Chef Claire said. "Maybe they'll get lucky."

"That would be nice," I said, then glanced at Josie. "Since you're spending the day skiing, do you mind if I borrow your phone tomorrow?"

"Knock yourself out," Josie said, then frowned. "I can't believe I got roped into going cross-country skiing."

"It'll be fun," Chef Claire said.

"Are you sure you don't need me at the meeting tomorrow?" Josie said.

"Oh, I'm positive," I said, laughing as I stepped into the dining room and was overwhelmed by the smell of chili and cornbread.

Chapter 8

Right after a breakfast of French toast and way too much bacon, I said goodbye to everyone, gave Max a hug and a kiss, then climbed into my SUV. It had stopped snowing sometime during the night, and the plows had done a great job clearing the main streets. As such, the drive back into the city center didn't require the white-knuckle treatment, and I was able to sit back and enjoy the images the thick, white blanket had created. Officially, forty-nine centimeters had fallen, just short of a record, and I briefly tried to convert the snowfall into inches but got a headache doing the math and decided *a lot* was close enough.

I followed the directions Max had jotted down for me, but after a few minutes, I realized I wasn't going to need them since the route was taking me right back to where we'd been yesterday. And although I didn't recognize the building's address, it ended up being right across the street from John Naylor's loft. I parked on a side street and walked to the corner where the two streets met. I glanced back and forth at both buildings, shivered as a gust of wind blew snow in my face, then wheeled around and headed inside. I glanced around the lobby and saw Abby sitting near the security desk checking her messages. She spotted me, put her phone away and stood up to give me a hug.

"You made it," Abby said, tossing her bag over her shoulder.

"Yeah, it wasn't bad at all," I said. "Did you know that Victor's place was right across the street from Naylor's loft?"

"I did not," Abby said. "Convenient, huh?"

"I was going to go with weird," I said, glancing back outside. "Do we need to check in with security?"

"Already done," Abby said. "Victor is on the fifth floor."

She led the way to the elevators, and I unzipped my coat and leaned against the back wall as the doors closed.

"What are Chef Claire and Josie doing today?" Abby said.

"They're going cross-country skiing with Max and the dogs," I said, laughing a little too loud.

"Really? How does Josie feel about that?" Abby said, frowning.

"She's...conflicted," I said, grinning at her.

The elevator came to a gentle stop, and I followed her down the hall. Abby pressed the buzzer, and a few moments later, Victor Rollins opened the door and beamed at us.

"Welcome, ladies," he said, gesturing us inside. "It's great to see you."

We exchanged brief hugs with him, and he took our coats and headed to the kitchen to make coffee. While we waited for him, we wandered around his loft taking the place in. It was bigger than Naylor's, and several original paintings covered a lot of the wall space. I glanced out the wall of windows at the building directly across the street and tried to figure out which of the lofts belonged to the photographer. I turned around when I heard Victor heading our way carrying three steaming mugs. I accepted the one he was holding out and took a sip.

"This is a really nice place. But I never would have figured you as a loft guy, Victor," I said, sitting down.

"Me either," he said, shrugging. "But Wilma talked me into it. And I'm glad she did. I love it here."

Wilma Firestone was Victor's girlfriend and someone I had also met during our previous adventure in Ottawa. She was an animal massage therapist who had been swindled out of a business deal by the former CEO of Middleton Enterprises, Joshua Middleton, who had been murdered during the conference. Both Wilma and Victor had originally been suspects, then cleared when I was able to piece together the identity of the murderer. Since then, Victor, formerly the COO of the company, had been promoted, and he and Wilma had moved in together.

"Where's Wilma?" I said.

"She's in the shower," Victor said. "She'll be out in a minute."

"I assume you heard about what happened at John Naylor's place yesterday," I said, making quick work of my coffee.

"Yes, we did," Victor said. "We saw all the police cars and the ambulance and knew something was up. Then we heard

74

about it last night on the news. It's so sad. Melinda was a wonderful person."

"You knew her?" I said, frowning.

"Very well," Victor said. "And Wilma is devastated."

"Where did you meet her?" I said, my neurons flaring.

"I think the first time was at a party. And then we started to run into her at a restaurant we like not far from here," Victor said. "After that, we got to be good friends with her."

"Was Naylor ever with her?" I said.

"She was with him a few times," he said, nodding. "But we kept our distance whenever he was around."

"Because?"

"Because I can't stand the guy," Victor said, scowling. "Some of his photos have done some real damage to a couple of my friends."

"Tabloid photos?"

"Well, they sure weren't school portraits," Victor said, heading off to the kitchen and returning with a carafe of coffee.

"We were there yesterday," I said, holding my mug out for a refill.

"Really? At Naylor's?" Victor said, frowning. "Can I ask you why?"

"We hired him to do the photo shoot for our marketing campaign," I said. "Naylor is buddies with our head of logistics."

"Interesting. How did he do?"

"Great," I said. "But someone broke into his loft and took all his camera equipment and computer. Everything we did yesterday is missing."

"And the cops think it might be the same person who killed Melinda?" Victor said, stirring his coffee, deep in thought.

"That seems to be the working theory at the moment," I said, then paused before deciding to tell him the rest of the story. "I'm the one who found the body."

"You're kidding, right?"

I gave him a weak smile and shook my head.

"I have to say that you definitely have a tendency to show up at the strangest times, Suzy," he said, laughing.

"Yeah, I really need to start working on that."

"How was she killed?" Victor said, leaning forward. "The news story was pretty vague."

"It looks like she was poisoned," I said. "The killer apparently spread a white powder on Naylor's pillows, and she must have ingested some of it when she laid down to take a nap."

Victor looked away for a moment, then back at me.

"So, that would mean Naylor was the intended target," he said.

"It certainly looks that way," I said. "Melinda was simply in the wrong place at the wrong time. At least that's what the cops are thinking."

"I knew it," Victor said, nodding. "Somebody had to be going after him."

"I imagine he's made a lot of enemies," I said.

We glanced up when we heard the bathroom door open. Wilma forced a sad smile and gave us a small wave as she approached. Abby and I both stood and exchanged hugs with her. She poured herself a mug of coffee and sat down next to Victor on the couch.

"How are you guys doing?" she said.

"We're good, Wilma," I said. "We're so sorry about what happened to Melinda."

"Thanks," she said. "I still can't believe it."

"Suzy was just filling me in on what happened at Naylor's yesterday," Victor said. "She's the one who found the body."

"You were?" Wilma said, frowning at me.

"Yeah, we had our dogs there yesterday for a photo shoot. We're featuring them in the Wags' marketing campaign."

"I see," she said, nodding. "But how did you happen to be the one who found the body?"

"I left my phone behind and went back to get it," I said. "It looks she went into the bedroom to take a nap. The police think she was just in the wrong place at the wrong time."

"Or maybe she got caught up in something Naylor was doing."

"Like what?" I said, my neurons flaring.

"Who knows?" she said, shrugging. "But since she worked for that sleazebag, I guess anything is possible."

"Absolutely," Victor said, nodding. Then he shifted gears. "Okay, since all the work you did yesterday has gone missing, I guess that means you're going to have to push back the marketing campaign. Which means we'll have to push back the product launch."

"No, I don't think so," Abby said. "We're going to reschedule the shoot, and unless something else happens, it shouldn't impact our schedule."

"You mean, something wonderful like Naylor getting arrested for murder?" Victor said.

"I doubt if that's going to happen, Victor," I said, glancing down when I heard Josie's phone buzz. "I should probably take this."

"Go ahead," Abby said, reaching for her bag. "I'll get started by going through some of these numbers with Victor."

"I always love it when I get excused from math class," I said, grinning at her, then answering the call. "Hello."

"Ms. Court?" the voice on the other end of the line said.

"No, this is Suzy Chandler."

"Suzy," Detective Billets said. "It's me, Shirley."

"Hey, how are you doing? I borrowed Josie's phone for the day."

"Well, since you were the one I wanted to talk to, that worked out perfectly," Shirley said.

"What's up?" I said, walking toward the wall of windows and staring outside.

"I'm sitting here with one of our techs, and it looks like we've got a hit on your phone," she said.

"That's great. How did you do that?"

"Don't ask me," she said. "But this kid we just hired is amazing. He was able to get a GPS location on your phone even though it's still turned off."

"I guess it's true that Big Brother is watching, huh?" I said, shaking my head.

"Actually, I think he's renting the guest bedroom," Shirley said. "Your phone is currently located at 112 West Johnston Avenue."

Stunned, I fell silent and glanced over at Abby who was in the middle of a focused conversation with Victor and Wilma as they studied a document.

"Run that address by me again, please," I said.

"112 West Johnston," Shirley said. "You sound surprised. Does that ring a bell?"

"At the moment, it's more like a cannon shot," I said, glancing around the loft.

"I'm going to need a bit more, Suzy," she said.

"112 West Johnston? Are you sure?"

"GPS never lies," Shirley said. "I'm familiar with Johnston Avenue, but nothing specific is coming to mind."

"Are you near a computer at the moment?"

"I am."

"Google the address and check the map," I said, rubbing my forehead as my neurons surged.

I stared out the window and noticed it had started snowing again.

"Holy crap," Shirley whispered.

"Yeah, weird, huh?"

"That building is right across the street from Naylor's loft," she said.

"I know," I said. "That's the weird part."

"Hey, hang on a sec," Shirley said. "How did you know that?"

"Because at the moment, I'm on the fifth floor of 112 West Johnston Avenue," I whispered.

"What? What are you doing there?"

"I'm in a meeting with Victor Rollins," I said.

"The guy who runs Middleton Enterprises?"

"That's him," I said, feeling the onset of a headache. "Wags has an exclusive distribution deal with Middleton. I don't believe it."

"I gotta say, I'm a little stunned, too," Shirley said.

"How precise is that GPS location?" I said.

"You mean can it identify a specific floor?"

"Yeah."

"I doubt it," she said. "But hang on. Let me ask my guru."

I waited a few seconds, then she came back on the line.

"No luck on that," she said. "Just the street location. Do you happen to know how many floors there are in that building?"

I closed my eyes and tried to remember how many buttons I'd seen on the elevator.

"I think it's ten," I said. "Plus, the floor the lobby is on."

"And the building is all lofts?" Shirley said.

"I'm not sure," I said, frowning. Then my neurons finally landed on an idea that should have been obvious. "Duh. Hang on, Shirley." I glanced over at Victor and called out. "Hey, Victor?"

"Yeah," he said, looking up from the document he was studying.

"Does this building only have lofts?"

"It does," he said, nodding.

"How many lofts per floor?"

"Four," he said. "Each floor is basically cut into four large squares."

"So, there are forty in total, right?"

"Yeah. Why do you want to know?"

Good question, I thought. I debated about going with the truth but finally decided to lie through my teeth.

"I've got a friend on the line who is moving to Ottawa and is thinking about buying a loft."

"Well, we highly recommend this place," he said, glancing at Wilma who was nodding in agreement. "And I think there are a couple for sale at the moment."

81

"That's great," I said. "Thanks."

"But tell her to bring a checkbook that can handle a lot of zeroes," Victor said, laughing. "These things aren't cheap."

"I'll let her know," I said, then focused on the phone. "Did you get all that?"

"I did," Shirley said. "How does your afternoon look?"

"It's pretty open. Why?"

"I think Bill and I should have a chat with you about Victor," Shirley said.

"It is kind of a strange coincidence," I said. "You think he might be involved?"

"I'm not thinking anything yet," she said. "But we're certainly going to take a look at it."

"Where do you want to meet?" I said, glancing at my watch.

"How about we meet you downstairs in the lobby in about twenty minutes?" Shirley said.

"You want to meet in the lobby? Won't that look a little suspicious?"

"We'll just meet you there, and then we'll find a quiet place to talk," she said.

"Like Naylor's loft?" I said.

"It's a crime scene," Shirley said.

"But you're the cops working the case, right?"

"Yeah, that's a good point," she said. "And Naylor had to move out until we're done with the place. Okay, I guess that could work."

"Good, I'd like to take a look from Naylor's windows and get a better feel for exactly what he might be able to see with the right equipment."

"*You'd* like to do that?" Shirley said, her voice rising a notch.

"I meant us," I said, embarrassed.

"Of course you did," she said, laughing. "Okay, we'll meet you downstairs in about twenty minutes."

"How hard would it be to get your hands on the list of residents who live here?" I said.

"I'm way ahead of you," Shirley said. "I've already asked my guru to get a copy."

"Great minds think alike, Detective Billet."

"Oh, let's hope not. I've seen your brain in action."

"Funny."

"We'll see you in a bit," she said. "Try to stay out of trouble until we get there."

"Sure, sure," I said, ending the call.

I glanced around Victor's loft and wondered how good a look at the place I could manage over the next fifteen minutes. But first I'd need a good excuse to be snooping around. I walked back to the living room where Abby and Victor were still in the middle of their numbers discussion. I stood next to them and listened for a few moments.

"You guys don't need me for this conversation do you?" I said, glancing back and forth at them.

83

"No, not really," Abby said, looking up. "I know this isn't your favorite part of the business."

"You got that right," I said. "I'm going to meet my friend for coffee in about twenty minutes."

"That's great," Abby said. "Is she excited about moving here?"

"Huh?" I said, startled by the question. "Oh, yeah. She can't wait. Say, Victor, I've got a few minutes to kill. Would you mind if I wandered around and took a look at all your artwork? It looks amazing."

"Not at all," he said, focusing on the document again. "Knock yourself out."

"Perfect," I said. "I'll give you a call later on, Abby. And don't let him try to start renegotiating the deal," I said, laughing.

"Where's the trust?" Victor said, glancing up at me with a grin.

It was a question I hoped wouldn't raise its ugly head over the coming days.

I took a cursory look at the artwork in the main living area, then slowly worked my way toward Victor's office. Over the next fifteen minutes, I saw lots of cool paintings and sculptures but didn't find a trace of my phone.

Chapter 9

By the time I left Victor's loft and reached the elevator, my neurons were on overload. I had hoped that my Snoopmeter might be willing to take an extended break now that I had Max to occupy a large chunk of my free-thinking time. But, apparently, I was wrong. And instead of envisioning the two of us taking the boat out for a relaxing day on the River or walking hand in hand through the soft sand in Cayman, I was zeroed in on the possibility that our dog toy distributor might have just tried to kill the guy who would be handling the majority of our marketing efforts. That couldn't be good news for Wags.

And from a mental perspective, it certainly wasn't doing me much good either.

The elevator reached the lobby, and I stepped out and almost ran into a large cardboard poster that was sitting on a stand just outside the elevator. I took a second to read it and learned that the building's annual Christmas party for the residents was scheduled for tomorrow night. Apart from thinking that the third week in November seemed early for a Christmas party, I didn't give it much thought, and I headed for the lobby and stared out the large floor to ceiling window behind the security desk.

"Can I help you?" the security guard said, giving me a once-over look that was a combination of *I don't know you*, and *I don't think you belong here.*

"No, thanks," I said, giving him a big smile. "I'm just waiting for someone."

"Where's the other woman you arrived with?" he said, glancing around the lobby.

"She's still up on five," I said.

"Right. Mr. Rollins," he said, studying his computer screen then tapping the keyboard.

"You keep a close eye on things around here," I said, deciding to toss a line in the water and see if I got any nibbles.

"The people who live here take security very seriously," he said, sitting up straight and throwing his shoulders back.

"And their privacy as well I would imagine," I said, placing my elbows on top of the counter and leaning forward.

"Of course," he said, nodding.

"Well, you're obviously doing a very good job," I said.

"Thanks for noticing. Who are you waiting for?" he said, his fingers poised on the keyboard.

"Oh, just a couple of my detective friends," I said casually.

"Detectives? Are you working a case with them?"

"Not yet," I whispered.

"What?"

"Nothing," I said, shaking my head. "No, we're just meeting for coffee."

"I'd kill to be a detective," the security guard said.

"Oh, let's hope not," I said, flashing him my best smile. "I couldn't help but notice the sign when I came out of the elevator."

"Yeah, it's not where I would have put the thing," he said, shaking his head. "I've already knocked it over twice this morning. But they wanted it somewhere where everybody was sure to see it."

"Isn't it a little early in the season for a Christmas party?" I said, recasting my line.

"Yeah, I suppose it is. But the residents made the decision a couple of years ago to move it up before everyone's schedules got booked. Most of the people who live here have a ton of responsibilities to deal with during the holidays, and since their Christmas party is always such a hit, nobody wants to miss it."

"The party is just for the residents?" I said, my eyes following a couple staff members carrying boxes of decorations to the far end of the main floor.

"Residents and their guests," he said, nodding. "I worked it last year. Guess who I met at the party."

"I'm gonna go with a famous Canadian," I said, laughing.

"Well, that's not much of a stretch," he said, grinning. "The whole party is filled with famous Canadians."

"Okay," I said, deciding to play along. "Hockey player?"

"Nope," the security guard said, cocking his head. "The Prime Minister."

"Really? That's impressive," I said, nodding. "What's he like?"

"He seems nice, but we didn't get much of a chance to chat," the security guard said, deflated. "As soon as I told him I didn't vote for him, he sort of wandered off."

"Politicians, huh?"

"Yeah. No sense of humor, right?" the guard said, then leaned forward and spoke in a conspiratorial whisper. "I hear that Paradis is coming to the party."

"The supermodel?" I said, surprised.

"That's the one," he said, grinning. "She's a good friend of Claudine Gilbert."

"She's a model, too, right?" I said, trying to recall some of the ads I'd seen her in.

"Yup," he said. "She lives in the building."

My neurons flared again, and I did my best to remain casual.

"Really? Well, knowing her reputation for living the high-life, she must have one of the lofts on the top floor. You know, she seems like someone who would need to have the best view possible."

It wasn't my best fishing expedition question, but it didn't seem to bother the guard, and he shook his head.

"Actually, Claudine's isn't anything like her reputation. She's very nice," the guard said, shaking his head. "Almost shy. Her place is on four, right below Mr. Rollins."

"Interesting," I said, staring out the window.

"Yeah, I guess you never know what somebody is really like until you meet them. Rule number one, right? Never believe what you read in the papers."

"That's good advice," I said, noticing Shirley's vehicle come to a stop across the street. "There they are." I tossed my bag over my shoulder and smiled at the security guard. "It was nice talking to you. I hope you get a chance to meet Paradis."

"How cool would that be?" he said.

"Way cool?"

"Exactly. Way cool."

I waved goodbye then headed outside and was greeted by the cold and wind that was producing mini-whirlwinds of swirling snow. I turned my collar up and fought the stiff breeze as I waited for the crosswalk signal to change. Bill and Shirley slowly worked their way across the street through the traffic, and we met on the corner.

"Hey," I said, bouncing on my feet for warmth.

"How about we skip the greetings and get inside?" Shirley said, her shoulders hunched.

I followed them into the Wilkerson then lowered my collar and unzipped my coat.

"Nasty," I said, stamping snow off my feet.

"Yeah," Shirley said, doing the same. "I hope it warms up and melts. It's way too early for this much snow."

Bill shook his head at our complaints then headed to the security desk. Moments later, he returned and pointed at the elevator. We followed him and rode to the fifth floor in silence. Bill slid a keycard into the lock, and the door clicked open. All three of us ducked under the yellow tape designating the loft as a crime scene then walked inside.

"Nobody's here?" I said, glancing around the loft that appeared identical to the way it had been yesterday.

"No, the techs will be back later today," Bill said, taking the large space in with a long sweeping stare.

"Did they identify the powder yet?" I said, removing my coat and hanging it on a hook.

"No, the lab is still working on it," Bill said. "Deadly and fast-acting baby powder is all we have at the moment."

I headed for the wall of windows and stared out at Rollin's building that was directly across the street. I felt Shirley and Bill's presence right behind me, and I glanced over my shoulder at them.

"How far do you think it is between the two buildings?" I said.

"It can't be more than a hundred feet," Shirley said.

"Nothing that a good zoom lens couldn't handle, right?" I said.

"No, it's not," Bill said. "We had the same thought last night."

"That instead of chasing people down at clubs, Naylor has started doing some work right here at home?"

"Yeah," Shirley said. "All Naylor would need to do is close the blinds and wait."

"Were you able to get a list of all the residents?" I said.

"We were," she said, handing me a single sheet of paper.

"This is great," I said, studying the page and recognizing several names. "Wow, talk about your heavy hitters. This is quite a list."

"It certainly is," Shirley said. "And they all share some interesting characteristics."

"Money and power," I said, nodding.

"They obviously all have the same address," Bill said, pointing at the document. "Except for the designation next to the street name. That must be the loft identifier."

"It is," I said, remembering the 5W I'd seen on Rollin's door. I glanced out the window and frowned. "Which way is North?"

Bill glanced out the window then pointed at about a forty-five-degree angle. I followed his finger then nodded.

"You got anything to write with?" I said, glancing around.

"I've got my pen and notepad," Shirley said.

"I need a bigger piece of paper," I said.

"I think I saw some in his office yesterday," Bill said, heading off. Moments later, he returned carrying a small stack of blank paper.

I accepted the paper and a pen from him and sat down in a chair in front of a coffee table. I sketched out a mockup of the building across the street that consisted of ten horizontal rectangles divided in half.

"Okay," I said, sitting back in my chair. "If we assume that Naylor was surreptitiously trying to film what was going on across the street, we can eliminate half the lofts since they're on the other side of the building."

I drew an arrow pointing North on the paper then checked the resident's list.

"Victor Rollin's loft is 5W. Fifth floor West."

"I see where you're going," Shirley said, nodding. "All we'll need to do is check the list and add the name of the resident to the right box on your drawing."

"It's a start, right?" I said, shrugging as I entered Victor's name in the box I'd labeled 5W.

"It's a great start," Bill said, sitting down next to me and grabbing the resident list.

"Do you see Claudine Gilbert's name on there?" I said. "The security guard said she lives right below Victor."

"The model?" Bill said, scanning the list. "Yup. There she is. 4W."

I jotted down her name on the diagram. We quickly filled all twenty boxes on my sketch, and all three of us studied it in silence. Eventually, I got up and stared out the windows. Shirley approached holding the piece of paper. She spent a few minutes studying the sketch then stared at the building across the street.

"Naylor would only be able to snoop on some of the lofts," Shirley said.

"Yeah, the fourth, fifth, and sixth floors," I said, nodding. "The line of sight just doesn't work for any of the other floors."

"You're right. The angle is too sharp on the others," Shirley said, nodding. "All you might be able to see would be heads and feet."

"Let me take a look," Bill said, joining us at the windows. Then he nodded. "Yeah, good call. But his view into the lofts on four through six is excellent."

"It is," I said. "And with a zoom lens, I bet Naylor would be able to get very up close and personal."

"He certainly would," Bill said, studying the list of residents. "So, that leaves those six lofts as our best guess at the moment."

"Yeah," I said, glancing at my sketch.

"Okay," Bill said, studying the resident's list. "Let's see who we're talking about. You've got George Theo in 6W, right?"

"I do," I said. "Who's George Theo?"

"He's a heavy hitter in the mining industry," Bill said. "He's fond of saying that, if it's in the ground, he'll find it and dig it up. And if you supply the water, he'll also throw in the world's largest swimming pool, on the house."

93

"Charming," I said, frowning. "In 4S, the same floor as the model, we've got Jeremiah Walters." I glanced back and forth at them. "Do you know who he is?"

"He's a finance guy," Shirley said, then glanced over at Bill. "That's right, isn't it?"

"Yeah, I think so," Bill said, nodding. "Maybe commodities. The guy is worth a fortune."

"On Rollin's floor in 5S is someone named Charlotte Evans."

"The Black Widow?" Shirley said, shaking her head in disgust. "I didn't even notice her name on the list."

"I'm sensing contempt," I said, laughing.

"She's been married five times," Shirley said. "And all of her husbands died unexpected, tragic deaths."

"Not to mention suspicious," Bill said.

"And I assume that all of them left her a tidy sum in their will?" I said, my neurons flaring briefly.

"She's done very well for herself," Shirley said, staring out across the street.

"How did they die?" I said.

"Mostly doing stupid stuff," Bill said. "Charlotte fancies herself as a bit of a daredevil and always expects her husband du jour to join in."

"Daredevil? So, she's a young woman?" I said, leaning against a wall.

"No, she's probably close to sixty," Shirley said. "But you wouldn't know that by looking at her."

"What sort of accidents did her husbands have?" I said.

"Let's see," Shirley said. "One died in a scuba diving accident. Another one was killed skydiving."

"Don't remind me," Bill said, shaking his head. "I caught that case. What a mess that was."

"His chute didn't open?"

"No, it didn't," Bill said. "Let's just say he did a very good job covering the landing area and leave it at that."

"Got it," I said, grimacing.

"Another husband drove off a bridge when his brakes failed," Shirley said.

"I guess things like that happen with cars, right?" I said.

"Yes, but not on a brand new hundred thousand dollar Mercedes," Shirley said. "Let's see, what else? Oh, one of them got shot while they were on safari in Africa. The Black Widow's story is that her husband went outside their tent one night to check on a noise they heard, and one of the guides mistook him for a cheetah."

"What?" I said, staring at her.

"Yeah, we almost got her on that one, but the guide's story held up," Bill said. "The shooting was eventually ruled accidental, and the guide is now living in a luxury condo in Boca. I'll leave it to you to connect the dots."

"Her fifth husband died in a parasailing accident in Hawaii," Shirley said. "Somehow the rope on the back of the boat that was tied to the sail came loose."

"Stern," I said, correcting her.

"I have no idea what he was like," Shirley said.

I stared at her, then shook my head.

"What?" Shirley said with a frown.

"Never mind. Not important. Hubby number five crashed into the ocean?" I said.

"He should have been so lucky," Shirley said. "He crashed into Diamond Head."

"Wow. And she's been a suspect in all five deaths?"

"She has," Bill said. "But as she likes to tell the media, she's just incredibly unlucky when it comes to love."

"And she's gotten very good at telling her story," Shirley said. "She actually has a lot of people feeling sympathy for her."

"Maybe Naylor caught her doing something on film," I said, glancing out the window at the loft in question. "He would have a great view from here."

"I guess it's possible," Shirley said. "But I doubt it. Charlotte's pretty good at covering her tracks. Who's in the other loft? 6S."

"Jennifer Thompson," Bill said, reading from the resident's list. "Doesn't ring a bell." He glanced at Shirley. "Does that name sound familiar?"

"No," Shirley said.

I grabbed Josie's phone from my pocket and searched on the name. I waited for the results to come back, then rubbed my forehead when my neurons exploded.

"I don't believe it," I said.

"What's the matter?" Shirley said.

"Jennifer Thompson is her maiden name," I said, a deep frown etched on my face. "It's Jennifer Bells."

"The ex-Foreign Affairs Minister?" Bill said.

"Yeah, and she's my boyfriend's aunt."

"And Naylor has quite a history with her," Shirley said as she looked at Bill. "Do you think that Naylor might have been trying to blackmail her?"

"Sure, anything is possible," he said, glancing out the window. "And he sure would be able to get a good look at what was going on inside her place. But why would he try to do something like that again? His reputation took a major hit for that incident at the club. He's still trying to dig out from it."

"Maybe she just decided it was time for some payback," Shirley said, then glanced over at me. "What do you think?"

"I don't know. But I think the answer to who killed Naylor's assistant is in one of those six lofts," I said. "We need to figure out a way to have a little chat with all of them."

"We?" Bill said, raising an eyebrow at me.

"You can't cut me out now, Bill," I said, grinning at him.

"Watch me," he said, not returning the smile.

"That's not fair," I said, pouting. "And you guys owe me one."

"Owe you for what?" Bill said.

"For solving the Middleton murder, what else?" I said, glaring at him.

"This case is different," Bill said, shaking his head.

"They'll all different," I said, my voice rising.

"No, I'm sorry, Suzy," Bill said. "You just can't walk into people's homes and ask them if you can take a look around. Especially those people."

"He's right, Suzy," Shirley said. "That building is filled with some very heavy hitters. And they're all extremely well-connected. I'm not even sure we'd be able to come up with a good enough reason to get into those lofts."

"Which means you need my help all the more," I said, smiling as I glanced back and forth at them.

"I know I'm going to regret asking this question," Bill said. "Exactly how do you think you can help?"

"I thought I'd start by interviewing all of them," I said, rubbing my forehead.

Bill snorted and shook his head.

"I think that's probably something we should take care of, Suzy," he said.

"No, I'm not talking about a cop interview," I said, grimacing. "I'm talking about a casual conversation. You know, just wander around and ask them a few questions in a social setting. Preferably after everyone has had a couple of cocktails."

"Are you okay?" Shirley said.

"Yeah, I'm fine. I just have a bit of a headache."

"I'm beginning to feel some pain, too, Bill said. "But mine's in a different part of the body."

"Funny," I said, making a face at him. "What do you think?"

"You're not going to get within a mile of those people," Bill said. "That's what I think."

"I'll bet you a hundred bucks I can talk to every one of them by midnight tomorrow," I said.

"No, I'd hate to take your money," Bill said, laughing.

"Chicken?"

"Chicken? Me? Okay, you're on. How about the loser buys dinner?" Bill said, unable to get the grin off his face.

"Sure. I'll make sure to come hungry."

"Okay, you're on," Bill said. "How do you plan on talking to all of them?"

"By going to the resident's Christmas party," I said.

"Resident's Christmas party?" Bill said, frowning.

"It's an annual event," I said. "And it's scheduled for tomorrow night."

"And you think you can get invited?" Shirley said.

"Well, the party is for residents and their guests," I said. "And between Victor Rollins and Max's aunt, I'm pretty sure we can manage to finagle an invite."

"You set me up," Bill said.

"Yeah, I guess I did. We'll let you know which restaurant we want to go to."

"We?"

"Sure. Max and me. Josie and Chef Claire. I can't very well go to dinner without them."

"You're bringing Josie? That's gonna cost me a fortune," Bill said.

"Hey, you should have taken the bet for the hundred bucks," I said, laughing. "You want me to see if I can get you two invited to the party?"

"Absolutely," Shirley said, vigorously nodding her head.

"I don't know about that," Bill said, frowning as he looked at Shirley. "Why would two cops be invited to a party like that?"

"Because you're a friend of one of the residents, why else?" I said.

"Which one?" he said, frowning.

"Victor Rollins."

"But I don't know Victor Rollins," Bill said.

"Sure you do," I said. "You interviewed him a couple of times during the Middleton investigation, remember?"

"Yeah, when I thought he might have killed the guy."

"Don't nitpick, Bill. C'mon, it'll be fun. Just think of all the celebrities you're going to meet."

"I'm in," Shirley said, glancing at Bill. "What is wrong with you?"

"It just seems weird to go to a party like that," Bill said. "We'll be off the clock and have to keep things social. What would I talk to them about?"

"That's easy. Just get them talking about themselves and nod your head a lot while you listen. Toss in the occasional *fabulous*, and you'll be fine," I said. "And if there's a lull in the conversation, talk hockey."

"Now, that he can handle," Shirley said, laughing.

"Gee, I don't know," Bill said, frowning.

"Paradis is going to be there," I said coyly as I raised an eyebrow at him.

"The supermodel?"

"I think you just said the magic word," Shirley said, grinning at her fiancé.

"Well, I suppose it couldn't hurt," Bill said. "What would we wear?"

"I'll find out the dress code and let you know," I said.

"Okay," Bill said. "But you have to promise to keep your snooping to a minimum."

"Sure, sure."

Chapter 10

After unsuccessfully trying to get into my party dress in the bedroom, I playfully swatted Max's hands away for the third time and headed for Josie's bedroom. She and Chef Claire glanced at me when I entered and grinned at each other.

"Let me guess," Josie said. "Somebody wanted to help you get dressed?"

"Yeah, let's go with that," I said. "He tried to follow me into the changing room at the dress store earlier."

"We noticed," Chef Claire said. "He's got it bad."

"Yeah, me too," I said, stepping into my dress.

"Well, I, for one, approve wholeheartedly," Chef Claire said.

"Yeah, I guess he's okay," Josie deadpanned.

"Funny."

"What did Victor say when you mentioned the party?" Josie said, sliding into the cocktail dress she'd bought this afternoon when the three of us had gone shopping.

"I didn't actually have to even mention the party," I said, turning around to look at myself in the full-length mirror.

"You merely steered the conversation in that direction, right?" Chef Claire said, also checking out how she looked in the mirror.

"Nothing gets past you," I said, grinning at her. "I just happened to mention that we had decided to stick around for an extra couple of days and that we were jonesing for a party."

"And then he just invited us all?" Josie said, turning around so Chef Claire could zip up the back of her dress.

"Not only did he invite us," I said, admiring the look of her new dress. "He apologized for not thinking of it himself. You look fantastic."

"Thanks," Josie said. "Is it too short? It feels short."

"Just be very careful when you sit down, and you should be fine," I said, laughing.

"I can't believe Paradis and Claudine Gilbert are going to be there," Chef Claire said.

"It's quite a resident's list," I said, brushing my hair back from my face. "And they're all rich and famous."

"Not the briar patch," Josie said, sliding a pair of heels onto her feet. "And you think one of them might have killed Melinda?"

"I think it's a real possibility," I said, glancing at the door when I heard the soft knock.

"Is everyone decent in there?" Max said, from the other side of the door.

"Come on in," I said, then gave him a quick kiss when he entered.

"Wow," he said, nodding. "You look fantastic."

"Thanks."

"All three of you look great," he said, glancing around. "Nice dress, Josie."

"It's too short, isn't it?" she said, frowning in the mirror.

"Not for me, it's not," he said, shrugging.

"Why doesn't that make me feel better?" Josie said, shaking her head. "But it is what it is."

"I just talked to my Aunt Jennifer."

"And?"

"And she's very excited about meeting you," Max said. "She wasn't even planning on going until I told her we'd be there."

"I can't believe she lives across the street from Naylor," I said. "Did she even know that?"

"She said she's been pretty much a hermit since moving in," Max said. "But the news about him being her neighbor didn't seem to faze her."

"I wonder if he's going to be at the party," I said.

"Who would invite him?" Chef Claire said.

"Maybe the model," I said, shrugging. "He does photograph a lot of them."

"Are the cops going to arrest him?" Chef Claire said.

"I don't think so," I said, shaking my head. "They're almost positive he was the intended victim. But they're definitely keeping a close eye on him. Did you take the dogs outside yet?" I said to Max as I slid an earring on then secured the back post.

"I did, and they are all now resting comfortably downstairs," he said. "I'm going to go change." Then he grinned at me. "You want to help me?"

"Go," I said, playfully shoving him out of the room.

Josie waited until I closed the door then spoke.

"You don't think his aunt is involved, do you?"

"Geez, I hope not," I said, frowning. "But her loft is right across the street from Naylor's."

"If we find out that he has been spying on his neighbors," Josie said. "I don't want him anywhere near Wags. Or us for that matter. That's creepy."

"I was going to go with perverted," Chef Claire said, brushing her hair.

"I agree," I said, nodding. "I guess there's only one way to find out, right?"

"How about you just try to relax and enjoy the party?" Josie said.

"Oh, don't worry. I'm definitely going to enjoy the party," I said. "And I'll be very calm."

"Because snooping relaxes you?"

"Exactly," I said, beaming at her. "Let's go."

We went downstairs to say goodbye to the dogs, then headed outside and walked down the driveway. Max was already waiting next to the SUV and enjoying the winter scenery. He was wearing a sport coat over a light sweater.

"You look nice," I said, kissing his cheek.

"Well, you said smart casual," he said, frowning. "Funny, but I don't feel any smarter."

"No, but you *look* smarter," I said, laughing. "And that's what matters tonight. Let's go. It's freezing out here."

I climbed into the driver seat, and Max hopped into the passenger seat.

"Do you have any idea what they're serving tonight?" Josie said.

"No," I said, backing out of the driveway onto the street. "But Victor said to come hungry."

"Like I have a choice," Josie said.

We made the short drive in relative silence, and I came to a stop under the covered entrance where several uniformed valets were waiting. I climbed out, stuffed the parking ticket into my bag, then locked arms with Max and headed inside. Another group of uniformed staff was waiting to take our coats, and I removed mine and handed it to Max. A woman holding an iPad approached.

"Good evening," she said, pleasantly. "Could I have your name, please?"

"Well, I'm sort of using it at the moment," I deadpanned.

The woman flashed me a weak smile and waited patiently.

"Maybe I better save that one for later," I said, laughing. "You know after everyone has had a couple of drinks."

"I'm sure that would help," she said, again flashing the smile.

"Suzy Chandler," I said. "Party of six and guests of Victor Rollins."

"There you are," she said, tapping the device. "The other two in your party have already arrived."

"Thanks," I said, squeezing Max's hand.

"Just follow the red carpet past the elevators. That will take you right into the ballroom. Have a nice evening."

She flashed me the smile for a third time then turned around to greet the people standing behind us. We slowly walked down the carpet taking everything in. The lobby area had been transformed since I was here yesterday, and I heard the sound of piano music ahead of us. At the end of the carpet, the noise level increased dramatically, and we stepped into a large room where over two hundred people were already in party-mode.

"This is nice," Max said, glancing around the room. "I'm glad we came."

"Me too," I said, squeezing his hand again. Then I spotted the security guard I'd met yesterday standing a few feet off to one side wearing a tuxedo. "Hey, how are you doing?"

"Oh, hi," he said, frowning as he tried to remember me then nodding. "5W, right?"

"Good memory," I said. "You look nice."

"Thanks," he said, tugging at his lapels. "I thought I should look sharp. Just in case." Then he got his first look at Josie. "Whoa," he blurted as if he'd been kicked.

"You thought you'd dress up just in case you happen to cross paths with Paradis, right?"

"Who?" he said, barely glancing at me before resuming his stare at Josie.

"The supermodel?" I said, laughing.

"Oh, yeah," he said, nodding in Josie's direction. "Is she a friend of yours?"

"She's my best friend," I said, glancing over at Josie who was chatting and laughing with Chef Claire.

"She's amazing," he said. "You think she might be interested in going out with a security guard?"

"Are you a dog lover?"

"No, not really," he said, shaking his head.

"Then I don't like your chances," I said, waving. "Don't work too hard." I looked at Max who continued to glance around the room. "Let's go grab a glass of champagne." I motioned to Josie and Chef Claire who followed us to one of the bars that had been set up around the room.

"Is that who I think it is?" Chef Claire said, pointing surreptitiously at someone on the other side of the room.

The rest of us followed her eyes and landed on a famous actor who was holding court with a small group of people.

"It is," Josie said. "He's shorter than he looks in the movies."

"I think most of them are," Chef Claire said. "Is he Canadian?"

"Who cares?" Josie said, laughing.

"Yeah, good point," Chef Claire said.

I grabbed four glasses of champagne and passed them around. I took a sip and surveyed the scene in front of me.

"Do you see your aunt?" I said.

"No, not yet," Max said. "You feel like mingling?"

"Actually, I feel like snogging," I said, laughing. "But I don't think we'd be able to pull that off without being seen."

"You're bad," he said, draping an arm around my waist.

"There you are."

I looked to my right where the voice had come from and saw Bill and Shirley headed toward us. I gave her a hug and shook hands with Bill.

"You guys look great," I said, giving both of them the once-over. "Bill and Shirley. I'd like you meet Max."

"Nice to meet you," Max said, shaking hands with both of them.

"And you remember Josie, right?"

"Sure," Bill said. "We had lunch at the Chinese buffet place."

"That was a good lunch," Josie said, nodding. "It's nice to see you again."

"And this is Chef Claire," I said.

"We've heard so much about you," Shirley said. "It's nice to finally meet you."

"You're the ex-girlfriend of the guy we put away for Middleton's murder, right?" Bill said to Chef Claire.

"Geez, not tonight, Bill," Shirley said, shaking her head at her fiancé. She turned to Chef Claire. "Don't mind him. He has a lot of trouble turning his cop-switch off."

"Don't worry about it," Chef Claire said, waving it off. "He's just a bad, distant memory."

"This party is amazing," Shirley said. "You'll never guess who we just talked to."

"I'm gonna go with a famous Canadian for a thousand, Alex," I said, laughing.

"How did you know that?" Shirley said, frowning.

"Really? He's here?" I said, surprised.

Shirley pointed at the man in question.

"How about that?" I said, glancing at Max.

"He's a very nice man," Shirley said, then turned to Bill. "Not that you would know that. You were busy with other things." She glanced around at all of us. "He was staring at Paradis the whole time we were talking to him."

"Oh, she's here?" I said, glancing around the room for signs of the supermodel.

"She certainly is," Bill said.

"I don't see her," Chef Claire said, also scanning the room. "What's she wearing?"

"Not much," Bill said.

"Why don't we find a table?" Josie said, looking around then pointing. "That one right over there is perfect."

"For a better view of the party?" Shirley said.

"No, it's on the appetizer route," Josie said, heading for the table and motioning for us to follow.

"Okay, Magellan," I said, shaking my head. "We're right behind you."

"She's joking, right?" Bill said.

Chef Claire and I looked at him and shook our heads.

"Just remember to keep your distance when she's eating, and you'll be fine," I said, sitting down with Max on one side and Bill on the other. "Okay, what's the plan?"

"I thought I'd drink, then eat, then drink some more," Bill said.

"You're pretty funny for a cop," I said, glancing up when I saw a woman approaching the table.

"I was wondering when you'd get here," Max said, getting up to give the woman a warm embrace. "You look great."

"It's so good to see you, Max," she said, glancing around the table before settling on me. "I'm Max's Aunt Jennifer. You must be Suzy."

"I am," I said, standing up to shake hands. "It's so nice to meet you. Please join us." I gestured at my chair. "Can I get you something to drink?"

"That would be nice," she said, sliding into my chair. "Club soda with lime, please."

111

"I'll be right back," I said, then headed for the bar.

While I waited to get the bartender's attention, I took another look around then waved at Shirley. I eventually caught her eye, and she joined me at the bar.

"What's up?" she said.

"I need some help putting a face to the names," I said.

"You sure you don't want to just take the night off and enjoy the party?"

"When are we going to get another chance like this to talk to all of them?"

"I know, but still," she said. "I hate putting you in the middle of an active investigation."

"We're just going to be talking," I said, accepting Jennifer's drink from the bartender and helping myself to another glass of champagne. "What could possibly go wrong?"

"Hang on a sec. I've got a list here somewhere," she said, laughing.

"Funny," I said. "I'll be right back."

I headed back to the table and gave Jennifer her club soda. I leaned over and gave Max a kiss. Jennifer started to get up from my chair.

"No, stay right where you are," I said, smiling at her. "I'll be chatting with Shirley at the bar."

"Try to stay out of trouble," Max said.

Josie and Chef Claire snorted. I made a face at them then rejoined Shirley. She took a sip of champagne and pointed at a table in the middle of the room.

"There's Victor Rollins," she said.

"So, I see. And the woman sitting next to him is his girlfriend, Wilma."

"I remember her from the Middleton case," Shirley said. "She's an animal massage therapist or something weird like that."

"That's her," I said, studying the woman sitting at the table with them. "Who's the woman at the table with them?"

"That's the Black Widow," she said. "Charlotte Evans. I wonder if she's flying solo tonight."

"Judging by the size of that rock on her finger, I doubt it," I said, staring at the largest engagement ring I'd ever seen. "But maybe she got it from one of her dead husbands."

"No way," Shirley said, shaking her head. "If Charlotte was on the market, she'd make sure everyone knew it. Well, what do you know?"

We both watched a large balding man I guessed was somewhere in his fifties sit down next to the Black Widow and give her a kiss. He ended up with his hand resting on her upper thigh.

"Silly man," Shirley said, shaking her head.

"Who is it?"

"That is none other than George Theo."

"The mining guy?"

"Yup," she said. "Well, at least he'll be able to dig his own grave."

"I definitely need to pay them a visit at some point," I said, returning the wave Victor was giving me.

I felt Shirley nudge me with an elbow and I followed her stare. Two extremely attractive and thin women were slowly walking toward the bar. In their heels, they were both close to six feet tall.

"That's Paradis and Claudine Gilbert," I said, doing my best not to stare.

"Yeah," Shirley said, shaking her head. "Genetics can be so cruel."

I laughed and snuck another glance at the women who'd come to a stop at the other end of the bar.

"Did you see how that space for them just opened up?" Shirley said.

"I did. It was like the parting of the Red Sea."

"They own the room," Shirley said, glancing around. "And this is a pretty tough room to own."

"Well, they certainly have most of the men's attention," I said.

"I hope they don't get their hopes up," Shirley said.

"What?" I said, glancing at her.

Shirley nodded at the two women. Almost hidden from view was the sight of Claudine slowly running a finger up and down the side of Paradis's thigh.

"That's interesting," I said. "I wonder if Naylor managed to catch them in a compromising position."

"Maybe," Shirley said. "But nobody would care. And the rumors about the two of them have been floating around for months. I think it actually helped both of their careers."

"Okay, that's all of the loft people except for the finance guy," I said.

"Jeremiah Walters," Shirley said, nodding at our table. "He's the one hitting on Josie."

I glanced over and saw the dark expression on Josie's face as she listened to the man whispering to her. Then she beckoned him closer and whispered something back in his ear. He flinched, then made a hasty retreat from the table.

"Wow, she's good," Shirley said, laughing.

"His biggest mistake was not waiting until she finished eating," I said, waving at Josie who shook her head at me then refocused on her nosh plate. "Let's go get an update."

We walked back to the table, and I stood behind Max and placed my hands on his shoulders. He grabbed one of them and gently kissed it. Jennifer watched it play out and beamed at both of us.

"Having fun?" Max said.

"Yeah, it's a great party," I said.

"You just missed Josie shooting down one of the richest men in Canada," Max said. "It was beautiful."

"He's a pig," Jennifer said, scowling.

"You're going to give pigs a bad name," Josie said, taking a bite of an egg roll. Then she focused on me while she chewed. "Did you know that there are several hookers working this party?"

"How the heck would I know that?" I said, frowning at her.

"I just assumed you've been snooping," she said.

"No, I haven't even started."

"He thought I was one of the hookers," Josie said. "Can you believe that?"

"In that dress, I guess anything is possible," I said, grinning at Chef Claire.

"He offered me five grand to spend the night with him," she said, popping the rest of the egg roll into her mouth.

"That's ridiculous," I deadpanned. "I'm sure you can get at least ten out of him."

"Shut it," she said, swallowing then taking a long sip of champagne.

"I'm going to go have a chat with Victor and Wilma," I said. "You'll be okay here, right?"

"I'm fine," Max said, squeezing my hand. "Aunt Jennifer and I are just catching up."

"I'll see you in a bit," I said, then headed for Victor's table.

Chapter 11

Victor and Wilma greeted me warmly then went straight back to ignoring each other. Apparently, they'd had a fight, and its effects were lingering. Victor introduced me to Charlotte Evans and the mining magnate, George Theo, who was finding it impossible to keep his hands off his fiancé. He did make time to remove his hand from her waist for a quick handshake, then refocused on the large section of bare back on display. As Shirley had said, I would have never believed she was in her sixties. The mining magnate was sitting behind Charlotte and oblivious to the look in her eyes that was one-part rheumy gaze, one-part death stare. She flinched a few times but tolerated George's wandering hands as she gave me the once-over. In angling terms, she had definitely hooked the prize fish but hadn't got him in the boat yet. When she did finally land him, I was pretty sure that George was going to have to find something different to do with his hands.

"Suzy, right?" the Black Widow said, giving me a small smile.

"Yes, Mrs...uh, Charlotte," I said, sitting down next to her. "Suzy Chandler."

"Chandler? I know a woman in Clay Bay with that name," she said, cocking her head.

"Yeah, she's my mom," I said, finishing the last of my champagne.

"I see the resemblance," she said. "How is your mother?"

"She's doing very well," I said. "Happy and healthy. You can't ask for much more than that, right?"

"Well, those two are certainly a good start," she said, laughing, then frowned when one of George's meaty paws landed near her right breast. "George, I'm out of champagne. Be a dear and get me another."

"Of course," George said, hopping up from his seat and glancing around the table. "Would anyone else like a drink?"

Victor and Wilma waved him off, but I handed him my empty glass and thanked him. Charlotte watched him leave the table then exhaled and shook her head.

"The things we put up with," Charlotte said.

"He does seem very fond of you," I said, grinning. "And that's an amazing ring."

Charlotte held the ring up to the light and examined it.

"It's a bit much, wouldn't you say?"

"Not if you're a glass cutter."

She laughed and sat back in her chair to get a better look at me.

"So, what do you do?"

"I run an inn for dogs in Clay Bay," I said. "And we've got a couple of restaurants. Now, we're getting into the dog toy business. That's why we're here. Victor's company is our retail distributor."

"It's an amazing concept," Victor said. "We think it's going to go big in a hurry."

"Fascinating," Charlotte said, already bored with the topic.

I decided to push the envelope a bit.

"We came to the city primarily to do a photo shoot," I said. "We're using our dogs in the marketing campaign."

"I see," she said, nodding.

"John Naylor did the photo shoot."

"Yes, Mr. Naylor," Charlotte said as a small grin appeared. "He does do very good work."

"Do you know him?" I said, forcing myself to remain calm.

"A bit," she said. "But mostly by reputation."

"His reputation as a photographer?"

"Primarily his reputation as a slimeball," she said, her smile widening. "But if people choose to put themselves in the public eye, I guess they should expect to cross paths with people like Mr. Naylor."

"I take it you're not a fan of his," I said, studying her face closely.

"I suppose if I gave him any thought, I probably wouldn't be," she said, shrugging. "But Mr. Naylor is insignificant."

"He is a bit of an acquired taste," I said, then decided to take a different tack. "Have you and George decided on a wedding date?"

"Not really," she said. "But he's taking me to Niagara Falls this week, so I imagine his plan is for us to elope. You know, surprise me with a spur of the moment sort of thing."

"Well, it is Niagara Falls," I said, shrugging. "A romantic spot, right?"

"I suppose. But knowing George, instead of staring at the Falls, he'll be wondering what was buried in the ground before it got dug up."

I laughed, and she glanced around the room, pleased by my response.

"Can I ask you a question, Charlotte?"

"Go right ahead."

"Why are you getting married again?"

She flinched, thought about my question for a few moments, then shrugged.

"I take it you don't buy into the concept of settling down with the person you love?"

"No, I do. Very much so. But I'm just having a hard time wrapping my head around the idea of being married six times."

"It's just a number," she said. "Mainly I do it because I hate being alone. And when it's all said and done, I do enjoy George's company." Then she looked off into the distance, and her expression went dark. "At least, I do for now."

The hairs on the back of my neck tingled, and I was glad to see George heading back to the table carrying three glasses of champagne.

"Any idea where you're going on your honeymoon?" I said.

"We're going to be sailing around the Caribbean," Charlotte said. "Just the two of us."

"Nice," I said, nodding.

"Yes, I love sailing. My first husband taught me."

I tried to remember if Shirley had mentioned how her first husband had died. As if reading my mind, Charlotte continued.

"He died in a tragic scuba diving accident," she said, glancing over her shoulder at George who was repositioning his chair behind her.

"I'm so sorry," I said.

"What are we talking about?" George said, passing the glasses around.

"We were just talking about our honeymoon plans," Charlotte cooed, glancing back at him.

"I can't wait to learn how to sail," he said, taking a big gulp of champagne.

"You don't sail?" I said, frowning.

"No," he said, shaking his head.

"How's your swimming?" I deadpanned.

Charlotte stared at me and gave me a strange smile that let me know she hadn't missed the message behind my question.

"Play nice," she whispered through a tight smile.

"I'm an okay swimmer," George said. "I've never spent much time on boats, but I'm sure this little lady will teach me everything I need to know."

"Just leave everything to me," Charlotte said, then spotted someone across the room. "Oh, George, I see the Crawfords. We need to go say hi." Charlotte got up from her chair and extended her hand. "It was very nice to meet you, Suzy. Please say hello to your mother for me."

"I'll do that," I said, returning her handshake. "You two have fun. And good luck with the wedding."

"You're obviously an intelligent woman," she said.

"Thank you, Charlotte," I said.

"Try to remember that it's never wise to follow the rumormongers. That's usually how people get themselves in difficult situations," she said, then waved goodbye to Victor and Wilma and headed off trailed by the mining magnate.

"What the heck did she mean by that?" I said, scratching the hairs on the back of my neck that were again standing straight up.

"With Charlotte, you never know," Victor said, then glanced at Wilma. "You still mad at me?"

"I'm getting over it," Wilma said.

"We had a fight earlier," Victor said to me.

"I hate when that happens," I said. "Nothing serious I hope."

"We were just arguing about something Wilma did without letting me know," Victor said.

"Let it go, Victor," Wilma said. "The selling price was fine."

"I guess we're going to disagree about that," he said, taking a sip of his drink.

"And it sold in two days," Wilma said, on the defensive. "I was getting sick and tired of dealing with it." She glanced at me. "It was an old house and required constant maintenance."

"I know that problem well," I said. It was true. Our place in Clay Bay was almost a hundred years old and regularly needed something done to it.

"You probably could have gotten more for it if you'd taken your time," Victor said, draining the rest of his drink.

"So, now you're a real estate mogul?"

"I'm just saying."

"Well, don't," she snapped, ending the conversation.

I waited out an uncomfortable silence then decided to change the subject.

"Have you seen Abby tonight?" I said.

"No, she can't make it," Victor said. "She called earlier and said she had some work to take care of. You guys were smart to hire her. She's good."

"She is," I said. "How well do you know Charlotte and George?"

"I know him pretty well," Victor said. "He spends most of his time here when he's not on the road. Charlotte only seems to be around a few months out of the year."

"She used to," Wilma said. "And then she met George. Now, she's here pretty much all the time. You know, making sure she gets him reeled in."

"I've heard some disturbing rumors about her," I said, going for casual.

"They're not rumors," Wilma said.

"We don't know that," Victor said.

"Five dead husbands?" Wilma said, raising an eyebrow at him.

"Maybe she's just unlucky," Victor said, rattling the ice cubes in his empty glass.

"You want to give her a shot and find out?" Wilma said.

"Not a chance," Victor said, laughing as he stood up. "Who needs another drink?"

We both waved his offer off, and he headed for the bar.

"It's a good party. I just wish I was in a better mood," Wilma said, glancing around. Then she frowned when she saw a man heading our way. "Ah, crap. Who invited you?"

"It's nice to see you, too, Wilma," John Naylor said, frowning at her. "Hi, Suzy. I didn't know you were going to be here."

"It was sort of a last-minute thing," I said. "How are you holding up?"

"I've been better," he said, shrugging. "Melinda's death is a lot to deal with. Especially since…well, you know."

"That it could have been you?" I said.

"Yeah," he said, glancing around the room.

"So, who did invite you?" I said, my neurons kicking into gear.

"Claudine Gilbert," he said, continuing to search the room. "Have you seen her?"

"She was at the bar earlier with Paradis."

"Oh, good. She made it in," Naylor said. "I was worried she might not get here given the storm."

"You're friends with both of them?"

"I am," he said, nodding. "And I'm supposed to do a shoot with them tomorrow."

"Runway?"

"No, they want some holiday *portraits*," he said, making air quotes with his fingers. "It should be a very interesting day."

"Got it," I said, frowning.

"I was supposed to do the shoot at my place, but the police still have it designated as a crime scene."

"How long before you can move back in?"

"They think it could be a couple more days," Naylor said. "But who knows? They're certainly taking their time."

"I'm sure they have their reasons," I said.

"Where are you hiding your camera?" Wilma said, glaring at him.

"Wilma, you really shouldn't believe everything you read in the papers," Naylor said, barely managing to make eye contact. "I'm just a photographer with an entrepreneurial bent."

"Bent's a good word for it," Wilma said.

"My days of tabloid photos are way behind me," Naylor said.

"Yeah, I imagine blackmail pays much better," she said, shaking her head.

"What are you talking about?" Naylor said, turning to confront her.

"You know exactly what I'm talking about," she said, returning his stare. "And now that poor girl is dead just because you tried to squeeze money out of some poor fool you happened to catch in a compromising position."

Naylor shook his head, then glanced at me.

"On that happy note, I think I'll go grab a drink."

"What a great idea," Wilma said. "Just leave."

"Enjoy your evening," Naylor said, shaking his head as he headed off.

"You were pretty rough on him," I said.

"He's the reason Melinda is dead," Wilma said.

"Victor said you knew her pretty well."

"We did. She was wonderful."

"So, who do you think Naylor might be blackmailing?"

"Just another of his targets, I'm sure. He's despicable," Wilma said. "I hope the cops are able to tie him to Melinda's murder. The man needs to be put down."

"That seems to be the prevailing opinion," I said, still trying to match her description of Naylor with my memories of the pleasant young man who'd done the photo shoot with our dogs. "Do you think that's how he's made most of his money?"

"That would certainly be my guess," Wilma said. "Tabloid photographs and blackmail. That's quite a resume, right?"

"I just don't get it," I said, shaking my head. "He seems like such a good kid."

"A lot of psychopaths do," she said, glancing up when Victor returned to the table.

"I brought you both a glass of champagne," he said, sitting down.

"Thanks," I said, accepting one of the glasses.

"What did I miss?" Victor said, glancing back and forth at us.

"John Naylor just paid us a visit," Wilma said, taking a long sip.

"Too bad I missed that," he said, glancing around the room. "I'd like to throw him off the building."

"Get in line," Wilma said.

"As you can see, we're not big fans of Mr. Naylor."

"It's pretty hard to miss, Victor."

"Yeah," he said, taking a sip of his drink. "I can't stop thinking about what happened to Melinda. We had her over for dinner at least once a month."

"She seemed like a nice kid," I said.

"She came from a tough background but had really found herself lately. She had a passion for film and photography," Victor said.

"She was saving her money to go to film school," Wilma said.

"And she loved spending time with us," Victor said. "She said that Wilma and I had restored her faith in love and that a loving relationship was possible." He reached out and squeezed Wilma's hand. "I'm sorry about earlier."

"Me too," Wilma said, leaning over to give him a kiss.

"Was Naylor involving Melinda in his schemes?" I said.

"No, I don't think so," Victor said, shaking his head. "The man is a total sleaze, but even he seemed to have a soft spot for her. She was pretty fragile."

"Like a baby bird," I said as the memory of her flitting around Naylor's loft flashed in my head.

"Exactly," Wilma said.

"She was just in the wrong place at the wrong time," Victor said.

"Horrible," Wilma said, tears streaming down her cheeks. "Just horrible."

I reached out and patted her hand, then stood up.

"I should get back to the table," I said. "Would you like to join us?"

Wilma and Victor glanced at each other and shook their heads.

"Actually, I think we're going to call it a night," he said. "Neither one of us is in much of a party mood."

"Yeah, I'm worn out," Wilma said, draining the last of her champagne. "It was nice seeing you, Suzy. Have fun."

"Are we going to see you before you leave town?" Victor said.

"I'm not sure," I said, getting up from the table. "We're sticking around for a few days since we're going to have to do another photo shoot. Do you and Abby need my help on anything?"

"No, I think we're all set," he said. "We're just waiting on the marketing materials so we can get rolling."

"I'll see what I can do to speed things up," I said, giving both of them a hug.

I waited until they left the table and headed for the elevators. Then I started walking across the room and caught a glimpse of John Naylor chatting at the bar with the two models. Then he glanced over at our table and shared an indifferent stare with Max's aunt.

I came to a stop in the middle of the room and studied Naylor closely.

"I don't get it," I said out loud to myself.

"That's because there's really nothing to get."

I turned toward the voice and flinched when I recognized the face I'd seen on TV and movie screens for decades.

"What?"

"I said there's really nothing to get," he said, smiling at me. "As soon as you realize that, life gets a whole lot easier."

"Yeah, I really need to start working on that."

He laughed and extended his hand.

"I'm Chris."

"Suzy."

"It's nice to meet you, Suzy."

"I love your movies," I said. "Well, most of them anyway. A couple of them were real turkeys." Then I flushed red with embarrassment. "Sorry. But you're always great."

"Thanks," he said, still smiling. "I think."

"So, that thing about how there's nothing to get?" I said. "What is that, some sort of Buddhist thing?"

"I guess it's something that Buddha might have said. But it came from the woman who wrote the movie I'm working on. I've been testing the line out all night to see how it works."

"It's a good line," I said, nodding.

"But not a good philosophy?" he said, raising an eyebrow.

"I'd have to give it some thought," I said, frowning.

"Try not to overthink it," he said.

"Who have you been talking to?"

"What?" he said, thoroughly confused.

"Nothing," I said, shaking my head. "Someone did tell me one time that life was just a series of individual, often random, moments connected by choices."

130

"Oh, that's good," he said, nodding. "Mind if I borrow that?"

"Knock yourself out," I said, grinning. "I'll keep an eye out to see if you use it in the movie."

"Tell you what, if I do, I'll give you a sign when I say the line. A little wink or a tug on my ear. It'll be our little secret."

"Perfect," I said, then had a thought. "Say, can I ask you a question?"

"Sure."

"I've always wondered about something. How much does an Oscar weigh?"

"Wow. I wouldn't have got that with a million guesses," he said, frowning. "Oscar weighs eight and a half pounds."

"Heavy."

"Yes, especially for a man my age."

"You're too modest. You look great."

"Thanks. Perhaps knowing that there's really nothing to get is keeping me young," he said, grinning at me. "Maybe you should give it a shot."

"I don't know, Chris. I'm not sure my brain would know what to do with itself."

Chapter 12

I got back to our table and sat down next to Bill and Shirley. Max and his aunt were still involved in an animated conservation that had them both laughing. Max noticed my return and beamed at me.

"Welcome back," he said. "Having fun?"

"It's quite a party," I said, nodding. "Where are Josie and Chef Claire?"

"They said they were going to mingle," Max said. "But I think Josie was hot on the trail of a dessert tray."

I laughed then felt a hand on my forearm. I glanced over, and Shirley leaned in.

"How was your chat with the Black Widow?" Shirley said.

"She's pretty spooky," I said. "On the surface, she seems charming, but there's definitely something bubbling underneath."

"Do you think she could have been the one trying to kill Naylor?" Bill said.

"I think she's completely capable of it," I said. "But I don't like her for the murder."

"Why not?" Bill said.

"It's strange," I said. "But I don't think she was interested enough in Naylor to waste the energy."

"What?" Bill said, frowning.

"I think she has to be personally invested in whatever she does," I said. "It's hard to explain. If she has killed all her ex-husbands, I'm pretty sure the reason she did it was just to see if she could manage to get away with it."

"As some sort of personal challenge?" Shirley said.

"Yeah, that's it," I said, nodding. "As the wife, she'd be the logical suspect, right?"

"Sure," Bill said. "At least at first."

"But she's always managed to meet the challenge and get away scot-free. And it was impossible to miss the way she dismissed Naylor as a human being. I don't think she did it simply because he was too *insignificant*. You know, unworthy of her abilities. Does that make any sense?"

"I guess it could," Shirley said. "Unless Naylor does have something damaging on her. She might like the challenge of getting away with murder, but if he tried to blackmail her and made her mad, she might make an exception just for him."

"I've been watching Naylor closely for the past half-hour," Bill said.

"Only because he's been standing at the bar talking to Paradis," Shirley said, laughing.

"Hey, I can't help it if that's who he chooses to spend his time with," Bill said, grinning at her.

"How does he seem to you?" I said.

"Sad and worried," Bill said.

"But not guilty, right?" I said.

"Are you talking about him being guilty of murder or blackmail?"

"Blackmail," I said. "He didn't kill Melinda."

"No, I don't think he did, either," Bill said. "But I haven't seen a trace of guilt from him."

"Yeah, I got the same impression earlier," I said. "I suppose he could be doing a good job of hiding it."

"If he is, then he's a very good actor," Bill said. "I'm beginning to wonder if somebody tried to kill Naylor for a different reason other than blackmail. Maybe he just rubbed somebody the wrong way."

"Like someone who was the subject of one of his photos?" Shirley said.

"Have you seen any tabloid photos lately that were credited to him?" I said. "He said earlier that he'd been out of the business for a long time."

"I wouldn't have a clue, but I really haven't been looking," Shirley said, frowning. "I don't follow the tabloids."

"I've got a few of our folks doing some research," Bill said. "But I don't think they've got any hits yet."

"A lot of the tabloid photos don't even have credits attached to them," Shirley said.

"Yeah, that one's a real needle in the haystack," Bill said.

"When are you going to let Naylor move back into his place?" I said.

"It's gonna be awhile," he said. "We're going over every inch of his loft again to see if he has something hidden that the person who cleaned his place out might have missed."

"Maybe he's got a jealous boyfriend or husband after him," Shirley said. "He does have a reputation as a player."

"Yeah," Bill said, nodding. "But we've dealt with a lot of jealous lovers over the years, and I've never seen one of them use an elaborate plan like the killer tried to use with Naylor. People who are in a jealous rage tend to use a more direct approach."

"You're right," Shirley said, nodding. Then she focused on her fiancé. "Hey, I thought we were going to take the night off."

"I think we failed," Bill said, laughing. "I'm blaming Suzy."

"Funny," I said. "Did you get a chance to check out the housekeeping angle?"

"We did," Bill said. "Naylor's building has a master contract with a company called High-End Housekeeping. They clean all the lofts. And they come in twice a week."

"Naylor has an assigned housekeeper?"

"He does," Bill said. "And she was there the day before Melinda died. She came at her regular time in the morning, did her thing, and was gone by noon."

"Did she change the linens in the bedroom?" I said.

"She did," he said. "And you saw how well the bed was made. I believe hotel-quality was the term you used."

135

"Yeah, I remember. And that means that Naylor didn't sleep at his place that night."

"He swears he didn't. Says he stayed with a friend," Bill said. "But maybe he passed out in the living room."

"It's possible. But I can't believe the housekeeper was the one who put the poison on Naylor's pillows."

"We can't either," Bill said. "But we had to check her out, and she came up clean. She's been Naylor's housekeeper since he moved in and loves the guy to death. A mother of six who goes to church every day."

"Not exactly a killer's profile, huh?" I said.

"Uh, no," Bill said, shaking his head.

"What about Melinda?" I said.

"What about her?"

"Where did she live?"

"She had a crappy apartment she shared with a roommate just outside of the city," Bill said. "And when I say crappy, I'm being generous."

"Apparently, she was saving all her money to go to film school."

"That's what her roommate told us," he said.

"What was the roommate like?"

"She was nice enough," Shirley said. "But really shaken up about what had happened to Melinda."

"What does she do?"

"She's a grad student," Shirley said. "Works a couple of part-time jobs. Wondering if she's going to be able to find a job when she graduates. All the usual stuff."

"What did she have to say about Melinda?"

"Just that they were pretty good friends but didn't see each other much," Shirley said. "She said Melinda worked all the time and usually ended up spending a couple of nights a week at Naylor's place."

"She and Naylor had something going on between them?" I said.

"Naylor says no," Bill said. "He thought of her more as a sister. Considered it his job to look after her."

"Do you believe him?"

"Yeah, I think I do," Bill said. "As far as she's concerned, I'm still convinced she just happened to be in the wrong place at the wrong time."

"Which leads us in a circle right back to who might have wanted Naylor dead," Shirley said.

"I hate when that happens," I said, staring off into the distance.

They both laughed and sipped their drinks in unison.

"So, you didn't find anything at Melinda's apartment," I said.

"No," Bill said. "But it's not like we did a major search of the place. We were just there to deliver the bad news to the roommate. And we got the heck out of there as fast as we could."

"What a horrible place that was," Shirley said, shaking her head. "I can't imagine living there."

"Yeah, the only thing memorable about it was the address," Bill said, laughing.

"666 Devil's Way Road," Shirley said, laughing along.

"You're joking, right?" I said, frowning.

"No, and if you ever saw the place, you'd understand why it's the perfect address," Shirley said.

"What's your next step?" I said.

"Keep going through Naylor's phone records and his financials. And looking for the missing cameras and computer," Bill said. "Or some sort of storage device."

"And hope that someone comes forward with some information we can use," Shirley said.

"Or wait until they try to kill Naylor again?" I said.

"That thought has crossed our mind," Bill said.

Chapter 13

We got back to Max's just after two, and Josie and I offered to take the dogs out. Chef Claire thanked us and headed for her room yawning, staggering slightly as she walked down the hall.

"She's buzzed," Josie said, grinning. "That doesn't happen very often."

"It was a good party," I said, watching Chef Claire fumble with the doorknob before finally getting the door open. "I'm going to throw some sweats on."

"Good idea," Josie said. "Meet you back here in five."

I headed to the bedroom to change clothes and found Max already in bed flipping through a stack of papers. He put the papers down when he noticed me slipping out of my dress.

"You want some help with that?"

"No," I said, cocking my head at him. "But tell you what, as soon as I get back you can help me out of my sweats."

"Deal," he said, continuing to watch me closely as I changed.

Josie and I took the dogs outside and stood shivering in the cold and snow. Chloe and Dente took care of their business straight away, but Captain and Al, apparently miffed that we'd left them alone all night, spent several minutes traipsing around the backyard and sniffing everything in sight.

"It's payback time," I said, watching the Newfie and the male Golden as they began roughhousing with each other in the snow.

"Yeah," Josie said, bouncing up and down on her toes and hugging herself. "C'mon, Captain. Let's go. You're not fooling anybody."

Captain paused to woof at her, then placed a giant paw on Al's head and dunked him in the snow. Al growled, then shook the snow off his head, and grabbed the Newfie's tail which started another round of wrestling. Despite the cold and the fact that it was way past our bedtime, we both laughed when we saw the dogs emerge from the blanket of snow that covered the backyard.

"Did you have a good time tonight?" I said.

"I did," Josie said. "Apart from that supermodel staring at me."

"Oh," I said, laughing. "Did Paradis take a bit of a shine to you?"

"Apparently," Josie said, shaking her head. "And I don't think Claudine was very happy about it."

"You little homewrecker," I said, gently punching her on the shoulder.

"I'm sure they'll get through it," Josie said, laughing. "Any breakthrough on who might be trying to kill Naylor?"

"No, but I did get a chance to chat with the Black Widow and her new fiancé."

"And?"

"She knows my mom," I said, shaking my head at the dogs. "C'mon guys, hurry up. It's freezing out here."

"Really? How does she know her?"

"I don't know. We didn't get to that," I said, frowning. "It's weird, but she sort of reminds me of my mom."

"You mean if your mother made it a habit to kill off her husbands?"

"Nothing gets past you."

"What would make someone get married and then spend all her time thinking up creative ways to get rid of her husband?" Josie said. "Captain, let's go."

"Personal challenge, I think," I said, shaking my head.

Chloe and Dente, apparently tired of watching the two other dogs playing in the snow, decided to join in. Soon, all four of them were rolling around and wrestling.

"Great," Josie said, shaking her head. "We're going to be out here all night. Captain! Go pee."

"Rule number one," I said. "Try to be smarter than the dogs." I whistled softly, and all four dogs stopped what they were doing and cocked their heads. "Snack?"

The dogs bounded through the snow toward the door. Halfway across the lawn, Captain remembered why he was outside, paused, then lifted his back leg. Al watched him, then did the same. We waited until they shook the snow off then headed inside.

"I'll handle the snacks," Josie said. "You go to bed."

"Are you sure?"

"Yeah, I've got it," she said. "Sleep well. And try to keep it down."

"Funny."

I walked into the bedroom still shivering and saw Max going through the stack of papers. He glanced up at me.

"What took you so long?"

"Al and Captain were staging a protest," I said. "It's freezing out there."

"I can help you with that," he said, pulling back the covers.

"I'm counting on it," I said, nodding as I undressed and slid into bed next to him.

"This is the best," he said, sliding an arm underneath my head and pulling me close.

"It is," I said, nuzzling the crook of his neck and shoulders.

"Oh, I forgot to mention that Aunt Jennifer invited us to dinner tomorrow night."

"Restaurant?" I said, glancing up at the ceiling.

"No, she wants to cook for us," Max said.

"Interesting."

"Interesting how?" he said, glancing over at me.

"What do you mean?"

"You know exactly what I mean," Max said, squeezing my shoulder. "We're way past coy, Suzy, so let's not go there."

"I'm just saying that it will be interesting to spend some more time with her," I said, deflecting. "I didn't really get a chance to talk to her tonight."

"She doesn't have anything to do with this Naylor thing," Max said, his voice turning protective.

"I'm sure you're right,' I said, my neurons flaring despite my best efforts. "Dinner sounds great."

"I have an all-day meeting tomorrow, so I might have to meet you guys there."

"That's fine," I said, nodding as I stared back up at the ceiling. "What time should we be there?"

"Eight o'clock," Max said. "Sorry to leave you alone all day, but I can't get out of this one."

"Don't worry about it," I said, then grinned up at him. "Saving the earth is a 24/7 job, right, Supermax?"

"You're really not funny."

"Disagree," I said, trying to squirm away from the tickling he was giving me.

"What are you guys going to do tomorrow?"

"Chef Claire wants to do another day of cross country. And I think Josie just wants to hang out and catch up on her sleep. I thought I might go for a drive around the city."

"A drive? Where?"

"No place special. Just drive around for a while. You know, just to clear my head."

"Good luck with that," he said, laughing.

"Hey," I said, punching his shoulder. "Be nice."

"You wouldn't be planning on doing a little snooping, would you?"

"No."

"Suzy?"

"I wouldn't call it snooping."

"Suzy."

"Yeah, maybe a little," I said, yawning. "But don't worry, it's nothing dangerous. I'm just trying to tie up a loose end."

"I really wish you'd stop doing this stuff," Max said, sitting up in bed.

"And I wish you didn't need to spend months away at a time in dangerous disaster areas," I said, staring at him.

He stared back at me, then eventually smiled and nodded.

"Fair enough," he said. "Just promise me you'll be careful and not do anything stupid."

"Sure, sure."

We settled back down in bed and resumed our previous position.

"You want to fool around, or are you too tired?" he said.

"I'm pretty tired," I said. "Maybe we should just wait until morning."

"Okay."

He leaned over to turn off the light then settled in next to me. Several moments of silence followed, then I whispered to him.

"Max?"

"Yeah?"

"You know, now that I think about it, technically, it's already morning."

"That is a good point."

Chapter 14

By nine in the morning, Chef Claire had already made breakfast for everyone, showered and changed into her ski clothes, and headed out the back door carrying her skis and poles with all four dogs excitedly bouncing at her feet. We looked out the kitchen window and watched her make her way to the cross-country trail that ran behind Max's house and led to a large park not far from downtown.

"She's a brave woman," Josie said.

"Because she's going cross-country again or because she'll be doing it while trying not to get run over by those four bruisers?" I said.

"Both," she said, laughing as the dogs knocked Chef Claire over while she was bending down to slip her skis on. "I'll clean up, then I'm going back to bed."

"You sure you don't want to go for a drive?"

"Do you need my help?"

"No," I said, shaking my head.

"Then I'm gonna pass," Josie said. "But you'll be back in plenty of time to go to dinner, right?"

"I will," I said, grabbing my keys off the counter. "Have fun."

I headed down the driveway and climbed into my SUV. I punched the address into the navigation system and followed the suggested route to the southern end of the city. It had started snowing again, and I shook my head at the early onset of winter that seemed determined to hang around. A half hour later, after making a couple of wrong turns despite the excellent directions, I located Devil's Way Road and drove past several apartment buildings and townhouse complexes until I reached the aptly numbered 666.

Compared to some of the depressed urban blight I'd seen in the States, it was in decent shape. But it was definitely the poorest section of Ottawa I'd ever seen. I parked in front, glanced around the empty street, and headed for the entrance. Just inside the alcove were a set of mailboxes. I scanned them, located Melinda's name next to another woman's, then pressed the buzzer.

"Can I help you?" said the voice through the intercom.

"Hi. I'm here about Melinda," I said, shivering as a gust of wind blew through a gap in the double doors.

"Cop?"

"No, I'm not a cop."

"Were you a friend of hers?"

"More like a friend of a friend," I said, bouncing up and down on my feet.

"What do you want?"

"At the moment, I want to get out of the frigging cold."

The woman laughed, and seconds later I was buzzed in. I headed down a long hallway on the first floor until I found the apartment. I knocked, and the door opened almost immediately. An obviously fatigued woman somewhere in her thirties stared at me.

"Are you Jane?" I said.

"I am. And you are?"

"Suzy Chandler."

"Who's the friend you were referring to?" she said, her arms folded across her chest.

"John Naylor."

She thought for a moment, then nodded and stepped back from the door as she waved me in. I entered, unzipped my coat and glanced around. Bill and Shirley hadn't been kidding. The place was dreadful.

"You want some coffee?" she said.

"Actually, that sounds good. Thanks," I said, then flinched when I caught a glimpse of what looked like a rodent's tail disappearing behind the fridge.

"That's Billy," the woman said, following my eyes. "Since the landlord refuses to get rid of the infestation, Melinda and I thought the least we could do was give the little guy a name."

"How do you know it's the same mouse?" I said, glancing down at the floor for signs of more.

"I don't," she said, shrugging. "But as long as I keep calling each one I see Billy, there's only one mouse, right?"

"I don't think I'd be able to keep my sense of humor about something like that," I said, removing my coat, unsure if I wanted to set it down. For the moment, I continued to hold it in my arms.

"Compared to what some of the other residents are dealing with, a mouse is way down the list," she said, handing me a mug of coffee.

I took a sip and nodded. "This is great."

"Good coffee is the one luxury item I allow myself these days," she said, leading the way to a small table next to the kitchenette.

It wasn't a long walk.

She removed a stack of textbooks from the table and closed her laptop. She set them down on the coffee table in the living room that, to be generous, was kitchenette adjacent. Jane noticed the look on my face and shrugged.

"Yeah, I know, the place sucks," she said.

"No, it's not…sorry. That was rude of me," I said, embarrassed.

"There's no need to apologize," she said, sipping her coffee. "It's unbelievably bad." Then she gave me a small smile. "But in about six months, this will all be a distant memory. Unfortunately for them, most of the other residents won't be able to say the same thing."

"You finish school in six months?" I said, glancing at the textbooks that all appeared to be science related.

"I finish my classes," she said. "Then I need to write my dissertation. But I'm going home to stay with my folks while I do that."

I decided that was probably a good decision on her part but said nothing.

"What are you getting your PhD in?"

"Biochemistry," she said, glancing at me over the top of her coffee mug.

"Sounds hard," I said, frowning.

"It is. My plan is to get into Forensics."

"Really?" I said, my neurons flaring. "Like criminal Forensics?"

"Pretty much," she said, nodding. "I've always been fascinated by it. I just hope I can find a job."

"Well, it is a growth industry," I said.

"Yeah, I suppose it is," she said, laughing. "What can I do for you?"

"I'm just trying to put a few pieces together. And I'm so sorry about what happened to Melinda."

"Yeah," Jane said, tearing up. "She was a really nice kid."

"I only met her once, but she seemed really upbeat."

"Most days, she was," Jane said, grabbing both of our mugs and heading for the coffeemaker. She refilled them and sat back down.

"Most days?" I said, frowning at her.

"Yeah, the past several months she'd been doing much better," Jane said. "But lately, she'd been…I guess preoccupied is the best way to describe it."

"I heard that she had a tough time when she was growing up."

"She did. Bad family, ran away a couple of times, then finally managed to get away for good when she turned sixteen."

"How did you guys meet?"

"I posted an ad for a roommate, and she was the first person who showed up," Jane said. "The first few months were pretty tough, but eventually she settled down when Naylor hired her. I think that job was the thing that turned her life around."

"Really?"

"Melinda struggled with depression," Jane said, drumming her fingers on the table. "But Naylor really encouraged her. She started taking photos and writing. And she almost had enough to finish her book."

"She was writing a book?" I said, toying with my coffee mug.

"Yeah, from what I could tell, she was very talented. I think Naylor saw something in her, and he spent a lot of time working with her to bring it out."

"Do you know him?"

"Naylor? Yeah, I met him a couple of times," Jane said. "He doesn't seem anything like his reputation. Melinda loved the guy."

"But not in that way, right?"

"You mean as lovers?"

"Yeah."

"No," Jane said, shaking her head. "No way. To her, Naylor was part father, part brother. And he was very protective of her."

"What was her book going to be about?"

"A collection of photographs and some of her poems," Jane said. "But she was insecure about her work and wouldn't ever let me see her stuff."

"That's too bad," I said.

"Yeah, I would have liked to have seen what she'd come up with. But the cops said that a lot of equipment was stolen from Naylor's loft. I hope all her photos turn up."

"She didn't have a camera here?" I said, glancing around.

"No," Jane said, shaking her head. "Neither one of us kept anything here of value. Every time I go out, even if it's down the street for milk, I take my laptop with me. She left most of her work and equipment at Naylor's place."

"Yeah, I guess that makes sense," I said, sipping my coffee as I glanced around the tiny apartment again.

"The concept for the book sounded pretty cool, and I loved the title."

I glanced at her as I took another sip of coffee and waited for her to continue.

"She was going to call it *Life in Moments: A Voyeur's Guide.*"

My neurons surged, and I visibly flinched.

"Are you okay?" Jane said, concerned.

"I'm fine, thanks. Where on earth did she come up with that title?"

"The concept for the book centered on the idea that life is simply a collection of moments, and if one pays close enough attention, you know, sort of like a voyeur might do, everything you need to know about somebody is right in front of you."

"Unbelievable," I said, exhaling audibly as I remembered my conversation with the actor at the Christmas party.

"Yeah, it's a great idea. She said she was going to focus on different people and get as many photos as she could and then present them in a way that told their story. Then she was going to write various personal essays and poems that tied the *visual narrative* together. Her term, not mine."

"Got it," I said, absentmindedly stirring my coffee. "She ever let you read any of her poems?"

"No," Jane said, shaking her head. "But it seemed like every minute she was here, she'd be in her room scribbling in her journal."

I massaged my forehead as my neurons redlined and my brain felt like it had been set on fire. I waited it out in silence and felt Jane's intense stare.

"Are you sure you're okay? You don't look too good."

"Just a bit of a headache," I said, reaching into my bag. I washed down a small handful of Advil with a sip of coffee and placed my elbows on the table. "Journal?" I finally managed.

"Yeah, she kept a very detailed journal," Jane said. "At least that's what she told me. I've never read it." She continued to stare at me across the small table. "What is it?"

"I'm going to ask you a question, and there's a good chance it's going to sound very invasive," I said, still vigorously rubbing my forehead.

"Okay," she said, now on guard.

"Is Melinda's journal here in the apartment?" I whispered.

"I'm pretty sure it's in her bedroom," she said. "You want to read it, don't you?"

I returned her stare and slowly nodded my head.

"Very much so."

"To what end?"

I gave her a small smile. It was a great question and one I should have been prepared for. I thought about it, decided to play it completely straight with her, then formulated my response.

"First of all, I'd like to read it because I'm incredibly nosy," I said, shrugging.

That got a small chuckle out of her, then I continued.

"And I need to give it to the police. There could be some clues in it that will help them identify who killed Melinda and is still probably thinking about killing Naylor."

"I see," Jane said, giving it some serious thought.

"Her journal didn't come up when you talked to the cops?" I said, then kicked myself under the table. "I mean, I'm assuming the cops have been here."

"They were here," she said. "They stopped by to tell me that Melinda had been killed, then they asked me the usual questions. What was she like? Did she have any enemies? Stuff like that. And then Billy ran across the guy's foot, and they got out of here as fast as they could."

"I think the cops are working from the assumption that Melinda had just been in the wrong place at the wrong time."

"And you're not?" she said, raising an eyebrow.

"I was when I got here," I said, finishing the last of my coffee. "And when the cops are done with the journal, I'd like to make sure that Naylor gets it. Unless you can think of someone else who should get it?"

She sat in silence for several moments, then shook her head.

"No, from what she told me, there's no one in her family she'd want it to go to. I guess Naylor would be the right choice."

She got up from her chair and headed into one of the bedrooms. She returned a few minutes later holding a thick notebook and tossed it on the table. It landed with a thud.

"Do you want to take a look at it before I go?" I said.

"No, I gave her my word," Jane said, shaking her head. "But if you do manage to find all her photos, I'd appreciate it if you could figure out a way to publish the book. She deserves at least that much."

"You have my word," I said, catching and holding her eyes with mine.

"Okay," she said, nodding. "Oh, there's something else." She grabbed a purse from the coffee table that dominated the floor space in the living room. "The cops dropped her purse off when they were here, and I found this." She held up a plastic key card. "I think it must be an access card to Naylor's loft. Are you going to be seeing him?"

"Yeah, I'm pretty sure I will," I said, staring at the access card.

"Would you mind giving it back to him?" she said, handing me the card.

"Not at all," I said, again glancing around the hovel. "Are you going to be okay here on your own?"

"Well, the thought of finding another roommate doesn't excite me very much," she said, shrugging. "And if I pick up some extra hours at work, I might be able to swing it on my own."

"The life of a college student, huh?"

"At this point in my life, I thought I'd be worried about paying a mortgage off instead of struggling to make rent for a crap-box like this. But what can you do, right? I work my butt off just to send a monthly check to Deep Quarry Enterprises."

"I'm going to get going," I said, getting up as I grabbed the journal and slid the access card into my pocket. "And thanks for trusting me with the journal."

"Please don't disappoint me," she said, leading the way to the door.

"I'll do my best," I said, pulling my coat on and zipping it up.

"And drive carefully out there. They're saying we might get another half a foot."

I waved goodbye and tucked the journal under my coat as I walked outside. I hopped into the SUV, tossed the journal onto the passenger seat, then used my navigation system to find the address of Deep Quarry Enterprises. Their office was also located on Devil's Way Road not far from Jane's building, and I pulled into their parking lot, parked in front, and went inside. I spoke briefly with the clerk at the front desk then handed him a credit card and instructed the surprised man to prepay Jane's rent through the remainder of her lease.

Chapter 15

Doing my best to keep my promise to play better with others in the same sandbox, especially the cops, I decided to give Bill and Shirley a call and let them know about the journal. I reached into my pocket, then cursed under my breath when I remembered that I hadn't borrowed Josie's phone before I'd left this morning. I turned onto a side street and pulled over. I punched the word shopping into the navigation system and located a mall not far from where I was. I followed the directions and was soon wandering around a crowded multi-floor structure searching for the phone store. I found it near the food court, stopped to grab a hot dog, then walked into the store and quickly polished off my snack as I looked at all of the phones. After the clerk told me that it would take at least a couple of hours before a replacement phone would be activated, I opted for a pre-paid phone and headed back outside. I finally remembered where I'd parked, climbed in behind the wheel, then spent a few minutes trying to organize my thoughts.

I called Josie first.

"Hey, you're up," I said.

"Yeah, I couldn't get back to sleep," she said. "I'm watching a bad movie. Whose phone are you calling on?"

"I bought a burner phone at the mall," I said. "I need a favor. Can you grab Shirley's number from your call history?"

"Can I do that while we're on the phone?" she said.

I frowned.

"I'm sure you can," I said.

"But you don't know how to do it, right?"

"Not a clue. Just call me back when you find it."

Seconds later, the phone rang, and I jotted down the number.

"Thanks."

"You need anything else?"

"Not at the moment," I said. "But I might need your help deciphering a journal later on."

"Journal?"

"Long story. Is Chef Claire back yet?"

"No. I imagine she'll be out there most of the day."

"Okay, enjoy your movie. I gotta run."

I punched the detective's number into the phone and Shirley answered on the second ring.

"Detective Billet," she said, barely managing to get her name out through what sounded like a bad head cold.

"It's Suzy. You sound awful."

She sneezed into the phone then coughed several times.

"You should hear what Bill sounds like," Shirley said, then blew her nose. "I think we have the flu."

"Well, I was going to drop by and give you something, but maybe it can wait a day."

"Yeah, not a good idea. Believe me, you do not want this," she said. "What is it?"

"Melinda's journal."

She sneezed several times in succession then blew her nose again.

"She kept a journal?" she said.

"Yeah, I haven't looked at it yet, but her roommate said she wrote in it all the time."

"You went to her apartment?"

"Uh, yeah," I whispered. "I just happened to be in the neighborhood."

"Nobody ever just happens to be in that neighborhood," Shirley said, adding annoyed to her list of maladies. "Why didn't the roommate say anything about the journal when we were there?"

"She said you didn't ask," I said. "And then a mouse ran across Bill's foot and you two got out of there."

"Yeah, he's a big baby about things like that," she said, then burst into another coughing fit.

"Any update on when Naylor is going to allowed to go back to his loft?"

"Tomorrow," she said. "We've done all we can do there."

"Any luck finding anything useful?"

"Nope," she said, then started sneezing again.

"Go back to bed," I said. "I'll give you a call tomorrow."

"Try to stay out of trouble," she said, then ended the call.

I put the phone away and looked out through the windshield and realized just how hard it was snowing. I decided that getting off the road was a wise choice and that the prospect of reading Melinda's journal in the warmth and comfort of Max's living room sounded pretty good. I drove back to his place and walked up the driveway. I found Josie stretched out on a couch with an open bag of bite-sized sitting on her chest.

"Hey, you're back," she said, sitting up and turning the TV off.

"Yeah, it's getting pretty nasty out there," I said, removing my coat and holding the journal up. "Feel like doing a little light reading?"

I sat down next to her and opened the journal to the first page.

"Her roommate gave this to me," I said, scanning the first entry.

"That was nice of her," Josie said, also reading. "I hope you thanked her."

"Yeah, I did," I said, turning the page. "I paid her rent for the next seven months."

Josie glanced at me, then frowned and shook her head.

"I probably would have gone with a gift card, but that's just me," she deadpanned.

I flipped through the pages of the journal that were filled with poems, short quotes, and various personal observations.

"Let's take a look at her last entry," Josie said.

"Good idea," I said, flipping to the page. "It's another poem. Life in Moments. The roommate said that was going to be the title of the book she was working on."

I placed the journal between us, and I popped one of the bite-sized as I read.

Life in moments, the gray voyeur says to me.
Just watch closely, and you shall see.
Everyone at work and play
Every day they lie and lay
Everything out on display
It's just life in moments, she says, you see?
And every day is free

Seeing is believing, the gray voyeur says to me.
Cut wide and deep, by her, not he.
Sun-filled skies won't stop the rain
Whispered pleas can't explain
Five hundred notes won't kill the pain
It's just life in moments, she says, you see?
And every day is free

"Okay," Josie said, looking up from the journal. "I've got no freaking idea what she's talking about."

"Me either," I said, frowning. "But we're pretty smart. We can figure this out, right?"

"I don't like our chances," Josie said, laughing. "The gray voyeur? What's that? Some reference to an older guy? Maybe she had a sugar-daddy."

"Anything's possible," I said, rereading the poem. "But the first verse reads more like someone is giving her advice. You know, trying to teach her about life."

"Yeah, I can get that," Josie said, staring down at the page. "Just watch closely, and you shall see."

"Then at the end of the verse the *she says, you see?* sounds like the voyeur is checking to make sure she understands."

"That would mean the gray voyeur is a woman," Josie said.

"I suppose it would," I said, frowning.

"How old is the roommate?"

"Mid-thirties, at most."

"Then I doubt if Melinda was referring to her," Josie said.

"No, that's not it," I said, rereading the poem again. "The second verse has to be a reference to some personal pain Melinda experienced. Can't stop the rain. Whispered pleas can't explain."

"Yeah, I agree," Josie said, reading. "Cut wide and deep. She has to be talking about some sort of personal loss."

"But what the heck does the five hundred notes reference mean?" I said, frowning.

"Love notes?" Josie said, glancing up.

"That's a lot of love notes to write," I said, laughing. "I probably would have gone with a gift card."

"Funny," Josie said, reaching for the bag of bite-sized. "Maybe it's a musical reference?"

"Now, that's a good thought," I said, nodding.

"Thanks. But five hundred notes would be a pretty short piece of music, wouldn't it?"

"Probably. Maybe. I don't have a clue. I'm confused."

"Maybe about some of the details," Josie said. "But from a big picture standpoint, we've got a young woman who's had something bad happen to her. And now she's being taught some life lessons by an older woman in the hope that it helps her get over it. But I don't get the every day is free."

"I think it means that everything you need to see is right there for the taking," I said. "All you need to do is look hard."

"And it's the last thing she wrote," Josie said. "That has to mean something, right?"

"My guess is that this poem was the one that was going to tie the theme of the book together," I said.

"Which means she was probably close to finishing it," Josie said. "What was she going to call it?"

"Life In Moments: A Voyeur's Guide," I said, reaching for another bite-sized.

"I can only imagine what those photos look like," she said, laughing.

"I thought the same thing when her roommate first mentioned it," I said. "I was envisioning some sort of collection of porn passed off as art. But now, I don't think that's it." I drifted off and let my neurons do their thing. "I think the voyeur reference is about someone who just watched life very closely. I don't think it's a sexual reference."

I flipped through the journal and scanned some of the other pages. I came to a stop when I landed on a page that had a single sentence written on it in a flowing calligraphic script.

"The best way I've found to hide a secret is to keep it in plain sight," I said, frowning at the sentence. "What the heck does that mean?"

"No idea," Josie said. "Keeping a secret in plain sight. Maybe it's about wearing your heart on your sleeve? That sort of reference?"

"No, I don't think that's it," I said, my neurons starting to bubble. "She chose her words very carefully. And she didn't say keeping a secret. She said hiding. Hiding a secret in plain sight."

My neurons exploded, and I visibly flinched. Josie jumped, startled.

"I really wish you wouldn't do that," she said, shaking her head. "One of these days it's going to signal that you've had a stroke, and I won't recognize it."

"Sorry," I said, staring off into the distance.

"Okay, Snoopmeister, talk to me."

"I need to get into Naylor's loft," I said, nodding.

"Man, you could have given me a thousand guesses," she said, laughing. "You think that Melinda hid some secret in plain sight at his place?"

"I do," I said, nodding. "But the cops haven't found anything."

"Well, a couple of problems with that idea come to mind," Josie said. "Like getting into Naylor's loft in the first place."

I reached into my pocket and showed her the access card Melinda's roommate had given me.

"You got a key to his place?" she said, frowning.

"Melinda's roommate found it in her purse after the cops dropped it off. She asked me to return it to Naylor."

"Which you're going to do, right?"

"Yes, just as soon as I'm finished with it."

"How do you know it's actually a key to his place?"

"Because it's identical to the one that Bill and Shirley used when I was there the other day."

"Okay. Problem number two. His loft is a crime scene," Josie said.

"Not anymore. I talked with Shirley earlier, and she said the cops are done with it, and Naylor can move back in tomorrow."

"So, just wait until tomorrow," Josie said, shrugging.

"No, I can't do that," I said. "There's still a chance that Naylor is somehow involved in this."

"You said yourself that you were sure he wasn't."

166

"I think things might be different now," I said. "Maybe Naylor is trying to steal Melinda's idea and wants to publish the book under his own name."

"That's a total reach even by your standards," she said, shaking her head.

"Yeah, it probably is," I said.

"But you still haven't figured out a way around the biggest problem," Josie said. "So, I don't like your chances of getting in there."

"I'm not following," I said, staring at her.

"You have to get past the security desk," Josie said. "You can't access the elevators to the lofts until you go past security. And they know all the residents very well, and all the guests have to sign in."

"Geez, you're right," I said. "I completely forgot. I'd probably have to show ID, and I really don't want my name in the guest register. That would be very hard to explain."

"That shouldn't be a problem if you have the cops with you," she said.

"I can't take them with me," I said.

"Why not?"

"Because they both have the flu," I said, frowning.

"Ooh, you were so close," Josie said, laughing. "Well, it was a good try."

I sat quietly fuming on the couch, fiddling with the access card. Then my neurons landed on something I hadn't expected, and I broke into a wide grin.

"I need to run out for a while," I said, standing up.

"In this weather?"

"Yeah, I'll be fine," I said. "I'm not going that far."

"Suzy," she said, her voice rising in warning.

"Relax," I said, heading for the door. Then I stopped and turned around. "Max said he'd probably be home in time to shower and change for dinner. If I don't make it back by the time you guys are ready to go, just head to Jennifer's place. I'll meet you there."

"And what do I tell Max when he asks where you are?"

"Just tell him I headed out to handle some housekeeping chores."

"Suzy, Max is the best thing that's ever happened to you. Please don't start lying to him."

"I'm not lying."

Chapter 16

I punched the address for High-End Housekeeping into my navigation system and followed the directions closely while keeping two hands tight on the wheel and my eyes fixed on the road. The snow continued to fall and accumulate, and I drove slowly. The weather was keeping a lot of people off the roads, and I pulled into the unplowed parking lot directly in front of a one-story building that was located in a mini-mall not far from Max's house. I stamped the snow off my feet, then headed inside where I found the place empty. I headed for the counter and tapped a bell sitting next to a computer.

"Oh, hi," a woman said, approaching the counter from the back. "I didn't hear you come in. I was actually just getting ready to close for the day. How bad is it out there?"

"Bad and getting worse, I'm afraid," I said, extending my hand. "I'm Suzy."

"It's nice to meet you, Suzy. I'm Georgette. How can I help you?"

"I'd like to talk with you about signing up for your services," I said, lying through my teeth.

"Certainly," she said, smiling. "I can help you with that. Follow me."

I walked around the counter and followed her into a large office. She gestured for me to take a seat.

"Nice digs," I said, glancing around. "You must be the boss."

"Yes, I am," she said, beaming. "I started the business several years ago. How did you hear about us?"

"A friend of mine recommended you," I said. "John Naylor."

"Oh, Mr. Naylor," she said, grimacing. "What happened at his place was a horrible tragedy."

"It certainly was," I said, nodding. "I hope things settle down soon."

"He called earlier," Georgette said. "Apparently, he'll be able to move back in sometime tomorrow."

"That will make him very happy."

"Unfortunately, his regular housekeeper, Svetlana, won't be back until next week. She was so distraught about what happened, I gave her some time off."

"That was very nice of you," I said.

"Well, she's one of my best people. And she deserves a break. But I'm sure Mr. Naylor will be more than happy with the replacement I'm sending over."

"I'm sure he will. When will she be coming?"

Georgette paused and raised an eyebrow at me.

"I only ask because we need to reschedule a photo shoot," I said, deflecting. "But we'll be able to work around your schedule."

"I see," she said, putting her glasses on and tapping her keyboard. "Let me just confirm that. She'll be there the day after tomorrow." She removed her glasses and set them down on her desk.

"Perfect," I said. "That should work just fine."

"Now, about your housekeeping needs. Are we talking about an apartment or a house?"

"It's a house. My boyfriend's house, actually," I said, giving her a coy smile. "He's not the best housekeeping in the world. And truth be told, neither am I."

"I see," she said, handing me a brochure. "Our rates and range of services are all outlined in there. Just take a look and let me know what you'll need. Or if you wish, you can discuss it with your boyfriend and give me a call in a day or two. We'll be able to handle everything over the phone."

She glanced out the window at the storm and frowned.

"I really should get going," she said. "My street always seems to be one of the last ones plowed."

"I understand," I said. "I do have one question though."

"Go right ahead," she said, sneaking another peek out the window.

"My boyfriend has some very serious allergies," I said. "It seems like he's allergic to everything."

"I'm sorry to hear that."

"So, if it's not too much to ask, would it be possible for me to take a look at the cleaning products you use?"

It wasn't my best effort, but it was the best I could come up with on short notice.

"You want to look at our cleaning products?" Georgette said, giving me her best what planet are you from stare.

"Yes, I have a list of everything he's allergic to. And a lot of them are commonly found in various cleaning products. I'm assuming that your staff picks up the products they use from here."

"They do," she said, nodding. "We standardized all our cleaning products a few years ago, and I keep all the inventory here."

"Smart. Buying in bulk from one supplier, right?"

"As a matter of fact, yes," she said, still staring at me in disbelief.

"We do the same thing with our business."

"Good for you," she said, shaking her head as she got up from her chair. "I suppose I have a few minutes. If you'll follow me into the warehouse."

I hopped up out of my seat and walked next to her as we entered an area that took up about three-quarters of the overall space. I noticed a wide variety of products on shelves, a large collection of brooms and mops, and finally spotted what I was looking for.

"This is one of our all-purpose cleaning products," Georgette said, handing me a plastic bottle. "All the ingredients are listed on the back."

"Geez, that's a small font," I said, squinting at the bottle. "I left my glasses in the car. You wouldn't have a pair of readers I could borrow, would you?"

She patted her pockets, then frowned.

"I must have left them in my office. Hang on, I'll be right back."

"Thanks so much," I said, calling after her, then whispered to myself. "Probably not my best moment."

I made a beeline for the racks of uniforms with the High-End Housekeeping logo embroidered across the left breast. I snatched one off a rack and stuffed it into my bag. Moments later, Georgette returned and handed me her glasses. I put them on, and my world turned fuzzy. I rocked on my feet, then stared at the bottle I was holding.

"Do they work for you?" she said.

"Close enough," I said, staring at three blurry bottles. "Yes, this looks fine." I removed the glasses and handed them back. "Are the rest of your products all from the same manufacturer?"

"They are," she said, fidgeting with her glasses. "I'm sure you'll find that all our products are all natural and environmentally sound."

"Great," I said, glancing around. "Well, that should do it. Thanks so much. Maybe we should get on the road, huh?"

"Yes, I think we should. It was nice meeting you, Suzy. Just give me a call after you and your boyfriend decide what you need."

"We'll do that. Drive safe," I said, waving as I headed back toward the entrance. "I am so going to hell." I chastised myself as I went out the door then shrugged. "At least it'll warmer down there."

Chapter 17

My original plan for the day had been to have a quick chat with Melinda's roommate, head back to Max's place to hang out with Josie, then have a nice dinner at Jennifer's. But the hand of fate had intervened, and I was now driving toward John Naylor's building wondering if my plan to get past security would work.

Some of you may not be buying my *hand of fate* argument, but how else do you explain the fact that in the space of twenty minutes, the roommate had turned over Melinda's journal, a collection of personal reflections I was sure held the key to what was going on, as well as the access card to Naylor's loft. And despite my personal resolution about taking a step back to let the cops take the lead and do their thing, both Bill and Shirley were flat on their backs in bed with the flu.

As I drove, I realized that my new resolution about trying to mind my own business had produced an unusual side effect. Several nagging questions bounced around my head that sounded a lot more like warnings than they did ways to solve the question of who was trying to kill John Naylor. I did my best to push them away and focus on the task at hand, but my neurons were relentless, and I frowned and gripped the steering wheel even tighter when I finally realized what was happening.

Wonder of wonders, when it came to my crime-solving efforts, apparently, the Snoopmeister was developing a bit of conscience. Now, instead of merely having to deal with Josie and my mom's carping, I was being forced to confront several nagging questions bubbling up from my subconscious. And if there's one thing I hate more than out of control neurons, it's when they start debating with each other.

Why don't you just turn over what you have, then get out of the way and let the cops do their thing?

I got this question from Josie and my mom all the time, and I quickly swatted it back with one from the other side of my brain.

Who knows how long they'll be out of commission?

They could easily end up being sick for a week, and the murder trail could turn cold by then. Besides, I needed to get home in a couple of days and couldn't wait around a week for Bill and Shirley to get back on their feet.

Take that, restless-leg neuron.

Fair enough, but why the need to sneak into Naylor's loft tonight?

Easy one. Since Naylor was moving back in tomorrow, this would be my last chance to take an unfettered look around the place. Whether he was involved in the murder or not, I didn't imagine he would appreciate me snooping around his loft for a secret that Melinda might have hidden in plain view.

And I already have plans to be in the neighborhood for dinner, right?"

Okay, now that one's a bit of a stretch.

Perhaps, but technically accurate.

But how do you explain the ruse you pulled on the owner of the housekeeping service? Not to mention the fact that you stole one of her uniforms.

I tapped the steering wheel with my fingers while I tried to formulate an adequate response. Unable to come up with anything convincing, I nodded and conceded the point.

Yeah, that definitely wasn't my best moment.

Which leads us to the real question. How are you planning on getting past the security desk?

Just watch.

I grinned and reached for my phone. I called information for the number, put the phone on speaker, then slid it into the dashboard holder.

"This is the Wilkerson. Security desk. How can I help you?"

I didn't recognize the voice but needed to confirm that the security guard I'd met during our initial visit wasn't working.

"Is Walt there?"

"No, he's off today."

"That's great."

"What?"

"I mean, good for Walt. He deserves a day off."

"I guess," the confused man said. "How can I help you?"

"I'm calling from High-End Housekeeping."

"Sure, how's it going?"

"Great. Look, we need to make a slight change to our schedule, so I thought we should give you a call," I said, choosing my words carefully.

"What sort of change?"

"We were originally scheduled to have one of our housekeepers there the day after tomorrow to clean John Naylor's loft."

"Hang on a sec," he said, then began tapping his keyboard. "Yes, I see it here."

"Well, he just called us and let us know that the police have given him the go-ahead to move back in tomorrow," I said, slowing down as I approached the building.

"Yes, I heard," the guard working the desk said. "So, what do you need to change?"

"Mr. Naylor has requested that someone come over tonight and get the place cleaned up."

I held my breath as I waited for his response.

"Tonight? In this weather?"

"Yes, our staff member says she's comfortable making the drive. And we're going to make it worth her while. The Wilkerson residents are very important customers, and we like to keep them all happy."

"I guess that won't be a problem," the man said. "She knows that she'll need to sign in with me before she goes up to his place, right?"

"She does indeed," I said, grinning.

"Okay, thanks for calling."

I ended the call, turned my signal on, then made a right into the guest parking lot. I parked, glanced around to make sure I wasn't being watched, then hopped out and quickly removed my sweater and jeans. Goosebumps appeared immediately all over my body, and I rubbed my arms and legs then pulled the High-End Housekeeping uniform over my head. It was way too big, and I had to cinch it around the waist with my belt. I shivered then pulled my coat on and took a quick look at myself in the driver side mirror.

"Close enough," I said, tossing my jeans and sweater on the passenger seat.

I locked the car, grabbed my bag, then headed for the elevator that would take me to the lobby. I glanced around when I got out of the elevator and noticed the first floor was empty. Everybody's probably hunkered down because of the storm I decided as I walked toward the security desk. The guard looked up when I approached the desk.

"Hi," I said, giving him my best smile. "I'm here to clean John Naylor's place. High-End was supposed to call and let you know."

"They just called," he said, sliding a clipboard toward me. "I'll just need you to sign in."

I scribbled an illegible Sally Jones on the page then slid the clipboard back. The guard stared at it, then glanced up at me with a frown.

"I can't read it," he said.

"Sorry. I have terrible penmanship. I'm Sally Jones," I said, flashing him a weak smile.

"Sally Jones," he said, typing the name into the computer. "I don't think we've ever met. You been with High-End long?"

"No, I'm pretty new," I said.

"Okay, you're all set," he said, smiling. "Don't work too hard."

"Thanks," I said, making a beeline for the elevators.

"Hey! Hang on a sec."

I froze in my tracks and shook my head. Busted. And I'd gotten so close to pulling it off.

"You mind doing me a favor?" the security guard said.

I turned around and walked back to the desk.

"What do you need?"

"We've been holding Mr. Naylor's mail down here. I was going to drop it off later, but since you're going up would you mind taking it with you?"

"Not at all," I said, exhaling audibly.

I grabbed the stack of mail that had a large rubber band around it, then headed for the elevators. When the doors opened on the fifth floor, I did my best lumber down the hall until I reached Naylor's loft. I slowly slid the access card into the slot and held my breath until I heard the click. I pushed the door open, flicked the kitchen light switch on, then hung my coat on one of the hooks. I walked to the center of the loft, glanced around, and noticed that the drapes that ran along the wall of windows were closed.

I decided that if Melinda had left something hidden in plain sight, either the bedroom or Naylor's office were the most logical choices. I started in the bedroom, turned the light on, and got a good look at myself in the mirror and shook my head.

"Wow," I said, staring at the baggy uniform that hung off me like a sheet accented with thick woolen socks sticking out of the tops of my work boots. "Sexy."

I spent several minutes checking inside the table lamps, behind the cabinets and dressers, and underneath the bed, all locations, I soon decided, that the cops must have already searched extensively. I took a look in Naylor's closet that ran the length of the bedroom and thought about doing a search through his clothes. But my conscience suggested that would be way out of bounds, so I turned the light off and headed for his office.

I slowly worked my way through the Japanese screens and frowned in the darkness as I tried to remember the office layout and location of the light switch. Then I took a step to my right and tripped over something. The clattering of metal on metal reverberated through the loft, and I ended up flat on my back buried underneath several unfamiliar items.

"Smooth," I whispered in the dark.

I got to my knees and reached up, fumbling for the light switch. Then the office was bathed in light, and I saw I'd tripped over three portable lights and a couple of reflector boards that had been in the far corner of the office the last time I'd been here. Other than that, everything else in the office seemed to be in the same spot.

I got to my feet and glanced around as I tried to formulate a game plan. But first, I needed to put the lights back to where they'd been before I'd fallen over them. I reached for one of the lights that had tripod legs and carefully positioned it on the hardwood floor. I grabbed another light, this one with a large, round base and picked it up. I turned it over in my hands until it was vertical and gently set it down on the floor.

I was about to reach for the remaining light when I stopped. Unsure about the sound I'd heard when I'd set the second light down, I picked it up again and turned it horizontally, then flipped it vertically. A soft scraping sound I assumed was also metal on metal was followed by a gentle thud. I rotated the light in my hands, then shook it. The soft rattle the shake produced set my neurons on fire. I sat down on the floor and examined the long aluminum tube that was attached to the heavy metal pedestal. I twisted the base with a grunt, then it gave, and I unscrewed it. Eventually, the pedestal dropped into my hands, and a small storage device fell out of the hollow tube and clattered on the floor. Stunned, I stared at the device then picked it up and tossed it into my bag.

"Who said clumsy doesn't come in handy?" I whispered.

I screwed the pedestal back on, set the light upright, then did the same with the remaining one I'd knocked over. I backed out of the office, turned the overhead light off, then made a beeline for the door. I was just about to grab my coat when I heard a loud knock.

"Crap," I whispered as I immediately felt the onset of a panic attack.

I stood still, afraid to move. Then I heard another loud knock and tiptoed away from the door. I had no idea who was knocking, but I was pretty sure I'd have a hard time explaining my presence after my housekeeping cover story was shattered. I made my way through the living area to the wall of windows then heard the unmistakable sound of an access card being slid into the lock followed by a loud click. Frantic, I scanned the immediate area, then remembered the door next to the windows that led to the outside patio. I pushed the door open, felt some resistance from the accumulated snow, but got it far enough open to slip through. I felt the cold immediately, and the wind whipped my baggy uniform like a flag flapping in the breeze. I held the door about an inch open with both hands and put my ear next to it.

"Hello?"

Security guard. What the heck is he doing here, I said to myself as a gust of wind whipped snow against the back of my head. I felt it slowly begin to trickle down my back and grimaced.

"Sally?" the guard called out. "Are you here?"

I waited out the sound of footsteps walking across the wood floor. A long silence followed.

"Hello? Sally?" Then he said out loud to himself. "She's probably in the bathroom." Then he again called out. "I forgot to give you this package when I gave you Mr. Naylor's mail."

I relaxed, came up with a quick cover story to explain what I was doing out on the patio, and started to pull the door open to head back inside the loft. Then another gust of wind hurtled a large clump of snow in my face, and I swatted it away with both hands.

Then I heard another soft click.

This click was the sound of the patio door closing.

I stared at the door and shook my head in disbelief.

"Please don't be locked," I whispered.

I turned the handle and pulled. The door didn't budge.

"Are you freaking kidding me?" I said as yet another sustained gust swirled the accumulated snow and covered my head and face.

I shook my head, similar to how our dogs shake off excess water, then peered through a small gap in the drapes. I caught a glimpse of the security guard setting a package down on the kitchen counter, then heading for the door.

I glanced down at the two feet of snow I was standing in, shivered as the thin cotton uniform billowed in the wind, and took back my previous comment about the benefits of clumsiness. I looked around the patio, then down at the ground about fifty feet below. I began shivering uncontrollably just as I heard church bells begin ringing somewhere in the distance. I counted the chimes, and when they stopped after eight rings, I realized that, in addition to being stuck outside five floors up in a snowstorm, I was also officially late for dinner.

I looked across the street, located Jennifer's loft and saw Josie and Chef Claire standing in the window staring in disbelief at me. I shrugged and gave them a small wave. Josie held up her phone. I reached into my bag and grabbed mine and placed the call. She answered halfway through the first ring.

"Whatcha doin'?"

"Shut it," I snapped.

"Nice outfit," she said, laughing. "What is that? Early lunch lady?"

"Funny. Are you going to help me get the heck off this patio?"

"Yeah, eventually," she said. "As soon as I can stop laughing. Hang on, Chef Claire wants to say hi."

"Looks like you're stuck out there," Chef Claire said.

"Yeah, the wind blew the door shut," I said.

"Sounds like a job for Supermax," she said, laughing.

"Well, he is able to leap tall buildings in a single bound," Josie said.

"Will you two please just shut it?" I said, frowning as my knees began knocking.

"Oh, I really don't like your chances," Josie said, again bursting into laughter.

"Is Max there?"

"Yeah, he's in the kitchen helping Jennifer," Chef Claire said. "Want me to go get him?"

"No, I want you to get me out of here," I snapped.

"Sure," Josie said. "Just one question."

"What?"

"How the heck are we supposed to do that?"

"Suzy?" Max said.

I glanced across the street and saw him and Jennifer staring at me through the window.

"Hey, sweetie," I said, giving him a small wave.

"Should I even ask?" he said.

"Probably not," I said, shaking my head. "But you need to get me out of here. I'm freezing to death."

"Okay, I'll be right over," Max said. "I have no idea what to tell them."

"Hang on," I said. "Give me a second to think this through." My teeth started to chatter when another sustained gust of wind attacked. "No, you better not. The security guard at the desk knows I'm here."

"And?" Max said, his voice calm and measured.

"And I'll probably end up getting arrested for illegal entry," I said, hunkered down and hugging myself. "Maybe for impersonating a housekeeper, too."

"It has to be better than freezing to death," Max said.

"Good point," I said, fighting an incredible urge to pee.

"Hang on," Josie said. "Wouldn't a high-rise like that have to have some sort of fire escape?"

"Yes, they do," Jennifer said. "Suzy?"

"Hi, Jennifer."

"Yeah, hi," she said, laughing and shaking her head. "I'm sorry, I shouldn't laugh. Do you see that box on the other side of the patio?"

"I do."

"There should be one of those collapsible metal chain ladders in there," Jennifer said.

"Hang on," I said, trudging through the snow toward the large box.

Halfway there, the wind gusted again, and the uniform billowed up over my head. I stopped, pushed it back down, and held it with both hands until the gust dissipated.

"Nice buns," Chef Claire said, laughing.

"That shade of red looks really good on you," Josie said, laughing.

"I swear, I'm gonna kill both of you," I snapped, then pulled the lid on the box up.

I reached inside and started to remove a large metal chain ladder.

"Just hook the top end over the side of the patio," Jennifer said. "Then just toss the rest of the ladder over the edge."

"Okay," I said, following her instructions. "Then what?"

"Then you climb down," Jennifer said.

"All the way?" I said, frowning as I stared over the edge.

"Well, I suppose you could drop in and say hi to some of the other residents, but I wouldn't recommend it," Jennifer said.

"Funny," I said, staring down at the ladder that was already swaying in the wind. "I don't think I can do this."

"Okay," Max said. "Just stay there, and I'll call security and ask them to come and get you."

"No, hang on," I said, inching my way toward the top rung. "I'll figure this out."

I got down on my knees in the snow and turned my back to Jennifer's window. The wind whipped my uniform again, and I shook my head as I tried to maneuver it back in place. Then I gave up all hope of modesty.

"Enjoy the show," I snapped, then ended the call and tossed the phone into my bag. I draped my bag over my shoulder and slowly inched my way off the patio backward onto the ladder.

My first few steps down the top rungs were relatively stable since I was still close to the patio. But the further I climbed down, the more the ladder began to sway in the wind, and I applied the death grip with my hands and feet. The snow continued to whip my face and exposed legs as I continued my slow, cautious descent. Halfway down the ladder, both legs began to cramp, and I snuck a peek down at the ground and saw Max and Josie standing right below the ladder. Max was holding a large blanket that looked extremely inviting. They both had concerned looks on their faces, but their expressions were nothing like the one I got from a man on the third floor who was staring at the woman right outside his window swaying back and forth like a fashion-challenged pirate wench swinging from a yardarm. After what seemed like a week, I finally reached the bottom step, felt my feet touch solid ground, then let go of the ladder and exhaled contentedly when I felt Max's arms and the blanket wrapped around me.

"Let's get you inside," Max said, gently leading me across the street.

"What about the ladder?" I said. "People are going to notice it."

"Jennifer said she'd take care of it," Max said. "How are you feeling?"

"I'm cold and grumpy," I said, grimacing as my leg cramps forced me into a limp. "And I really need to pee."

"Hang on, we're almost there," he said, pulling me closer to him.

"Max?"

"Yeah?"

"Are you mad at me?"

"Oh, yeah. I'm furious."

"You're not showing it," I said, glancing over at him.

"Don't worry, I will."

Chapter 18

Jennifer greeted me at the door with a steaming mug of hot chocolate, then led me to a bathroom. I noticed a thick sweater and a pair of sweats sitting on top of a hamper near the shower.

"Take a nice long, hot shower," she said. "That should do the trick."

"Thanks," I said, staring at the accumulation of snow in my hair that looked like white cotton candy. "I'm such an idiot."

"Don't worry," she said, laughing. "I won't tell."

"But what about the ladder?"

"It's already taken care of," she said. "Get in the shower. Now. When you're back to normal, we'll eat dinner. I hope you like Thai food."

"I love Thai food," I said, smiling at her. "Thank you."

"Hey, it's the least I can do. I've never seen Max this happy."

"I don't think he's very happy at the moment," I said, pulling the snow-covered uniform over my head.

"I'm sure he'll eventually find the humor in it," Jennifer said, heading for the door. "I know it didn't take me long."

I heard her laughing as she walked away.

"Everybody's a comedian," I said as I removed the rest of my clothes and stepped into the shower.

Fifteen minutes later, I was warm and dry, fully clothed, and really hungry. I headed into the living area and saw Max and Jennifer in the kitchen. I gave him a hug and a kiss, apologized again, then joined Josie and Chef Claire who were sitting near the windows staring out at the snow that continued to fall.

"She's alive," Josie said, patting the couch next to her.

"No thanks to you," I said, gently punching her on the shoulder.

"Hey, I was right there to catch you if you happened to fall," she said. "Or at least give it my best shot."

I glanced out the window and frowned.

"What happened to the ladder?"

"Naylor showed up a few minutes ago and pulled it up," Chef Claire said. "I think Jennifer called him."

"Why would she do that?" I said, glancing into the kitchen.

"She's Canadian," Chef Claire said, shrugging. "I guess it was the neighborly thing to do."

"Weird," I said, shaking my head.

"No, what was weird was the sight of you on that ladder," Josie said, glancing over at me before taking a sip of wine. "At least you got your annual workout in."

"You're really not funny," I said.

"Disagree."

"Dinner is served," Jennifer called.

We hopped to our feet and sat down at the table. Jennifer started us off with a Thai red-curry soup that was a total knee-buckler. I was reaching for the ladle to help myself to seconds when the doorbell chimed. Jennifer got up and went to the door. Moments later, she returned with John Naylor by her side.

"Good evening, everyone," Naylor said, glancing around the table.

"When I called Mr. Naylor about the ladder, I decided to invite him to dinner," Jennifer said, answering the question that was rolling around in all our heads. "I imagine he has a few questions he'd like to ask Suzy. Have a seat. We're just getting started."

She headed for the kitchen, grabbed a new place setting and arranged it in front of Naylor. He served himself and tasted the soup.

"Fantastic," he said, nodding. Then he glanced down the table at me. "You want to fill me in?"

"It might take a while," I said.

"Oh, I'd be shocked if it didn't," Naylor said, baffled but, so far, not showing any anger.

I started slowly by outlining my visit to Melinda's roommate, discussed the journal and how I'd come into possession of the access card to his loft, then briefly covered the housekeeping ruse I'd used to get past security. Naylor, along with everyone else, listened closely as they sipped soup, then I paused to focus on my bowl and waited for the inevitable questions.

"Melinda was working on a book?" Naylor said.

"Yes," I said, nodding as I sipped the red-curry broth.

"She never mentioned it. And you thought she had hidden something in my loft?"

"Yes."

"So, you thought you'd just go in and take a look around?" Naylor said, showing his first trace of anger.

"Yeah," I said, nodding at him. "I'm sorry, John. I got a little over my skis on that one."

Josie and Chef Claire snorted. I scowled at them, and they went back to their soup not even bothering to hide their grins.

"I would certainly say so," Naylor said. "And you managed to get yourself into my loft and then got locked outside on the patio?"

"Yeah, that's pretty much it," I said, pushing my empty bowl away. "I'm really sorry, John. I just got carried away trying to figure out what's going on around here."

"Why on earth would you do that?" Naylor said.

"Because it's what I do," I said, glancing back and forth between him and Max.

"I see," Naylor said, frowning. "What makes you think Melinda hid something at my place?"

"She made a few cryptic comments in her journal," I said, accepting the platter of rice Josie was holding out. "So, I thought I should test my theory out."

"Without consulting me?" Naylor said, spooning curry onto his plate.

"Yeah," I said, exhaling.

"Because you thought I might be involved, right?"

"The thought did cross my mind," I said, shrugging.

"I'm never going to live this reputation down," Naylor said, tapping his fork on the side of his plate. "Maybe I should just go back to shooting for the tabloids."

"No, don't do that," Jennifer said.

"So, what do you think she might have hidden in my loft?" Naylor said, turning back to me.

"This," I said, reaching into my bag and tossing the small storage device on the table.

"You found that in my loft?" Naylor said, staring at it.

"I did."

"Where?"

"It was stuffed inside one of the lights you use for your photo shoots. It was inside the leg of the one with the pedestal bottom."

"What's on it?" Naylor said, picking the storage device up and examining it.

"I have no idea," I said. "I haven't had a chance to look at it yet. Have you seen that before?"

"Never," Naylor said, shaking his head.

I was convinced he wasn't lying and my neurons flared for a moment then settled down. I began working my way through a very spicy Panang curry and rice.

"Maybe we should take a look at it after dinner," Jennifer said. "I'm intrigued."

"Me too," Naylor said, setting the device down. "This curry is amazing."

"Thanks," Jennifer said, smiling at him. "I'm glad you like it."

We finished our meal in relative silence, and I remained worried about how angry Max was with me. Then he leaned over, whispered in my ear for me to please pass the rice and squeezed my upper thigh hard. I nuzzled his neck.

"Have you forgiven me?" I whispered.

"No."

"But you will, right?"

"Maybe."

"That's harsh," I said, laughing.

"I do have a question."

"Go ahead."

"Of all the dumb things you've ever done, where does this one rank?"

I thought about it, then slid a forkful of curry into my mouth.

"It probably doesn't even crack the top ten."

"Yeah, that's what I was afraid of."

Chapter 19

After dinner, we sat down in the living room and got comfortable while Jennifer and Max, after refusing our offers of help, did the dishes. We sipped wine, made small talk, and tried to come up with a new date to redo the photo shoot with the dogs. Jennifer entered the room carrying a laptop, and she sat down and began fiddling with the connections.

"I thought we'd go through whatever is on that thing on the TV," she said, nodding at the large flat screen attached to a wall.

I handed her the storage device and sat back on the couch next to Max. Moments later, an image appeared on the TV I assumed was the book cover Melinda had planned to use.

"You want to drive?" Jennifer said, tossing me the remote then settling into a large overstuffed chair.

"Sure," I said, glancing around. "Is everybody ready?"

Everyone nodded and stared up at the screen. I clicked the remote, and the image changed to a photo of a woman sitting on a park bench in the middle of a heavy snowstorm. She was feeding peanuts to the squirrels and was covered in snow.

"A relative of yours?" Josie deadpanned as she glanced over at me.

"Shut it," I said, advancing to the next photo.

It was the same woman, and I clicked through a series of a dozen photos of the same scene.

"Life in moments," I said, nodding.

"Melinda had such a good eye," Naylor said. "Did you see all the subtle changes in the woman's expression?"

"I did," I said.

"It's very good," Jennifer said. "You really didn't know she was working on a book?"

"No, she was very evasive about what she was working on," Naylor said. "I imagine she wanted to surprise me."

"But you helped her out, right?" I said.

"Sure, especially when she first started working for me," he said. "But she picked everything up in a hurry."

I pressed the remote, and an image of Charlotte Evans appeared on the screen. She was sitting down and stroking a cat that was sitting on her lap.

"The Black Widow," Naylor said. "Why on earth would Melinda be taking photos of her?"

"I don't think that's the question you should be asking," Jennifer said, staring up at the screen.

"What do you mean?" Naylor said.

"Take a good look at it," Jennifer said.

"Wow," Naylor whispered eventually. "It looks like it was shot from across the street."

"Not just across the street," Jennifer said. "If I was going to guess, I'd say it was taken from your loft."

"What the heck was Melinda doing?" Naylor said, motioning for me to continue.

I quickly went through a couple dozen photos of Charlotte in her loft, sometimes alone, sometimes with George Theo, the mining magnate.

"Oh, this is not good," Naylor said.

"But it wasn't you taking the pictures, right?" Jennifer said, glancing at Naylor.

"No way," he said, shaking his head. "You have my word."

I continued to work my way through the photos, and we studied sets of several other people in various outdoor settings.

"She did great work," Max said. "But why would she feel the need to hide them from me?"

"I don't have a clue," I said, clicking the remote and flinching. I heard everyone in the room gasp. "No, hang on. I take that back."

"Uh-oh," Naylor said, shaking his head at the image.

"Oh, boy," Jennifer said. "Okay, I guess that blows our cover."

I stared up at the photo of Jennifer and Naylor lip-locked in a passionate kiss on the very couch Max and I were sitting on.

"Aunt Jennifer?"

"Yes, Max?"

"Do you have something you'd like to tell me?" Max said, grinning at his aunt.

"Well, a picture is worth a thousand words," she said, shrugging.

"Isn't he a little young for you?" Max said. "No offense, John."

"Hey," Naylor said. "If the situation were reversed, and I was the older one, nobody would say a word about our age difference."

"Well put," Jennifer said to Naylor.

"Yeah, you're right. Sorry," Max said, nodding. "How long have you two been an item?"

"We started a week after the incident at the club. Right after I resigned," she said.

"Even though everyone was convinced John was behind the whole thing?" Max said, glancing at Naylor.

"How many times do I have to tell you? I wasn't involved," Naylor said. "I'd never do anything like that to anyone, much less Jennifer."

"And he managed to convince you he was innocent?" Max said.

"He did," Jennifer said. "And after he was able to actually prove it, our relationship really took off from there."

"What sort of proof?" Max said.

"I've got some photos. And some video with sound," Naylor said, shrugging.

"Then why haven't you gone public with it?" Max said, glancing back and forth at them.

"Because I'm saving it for my book," Jennifer said, getting up and sitting down next to Naylor. She leaned her head against his shoulder and looked up at him. "It's nice to finally be able to let people in on our little secret."

"It is," Naylor said, then frowned.

"What's the matter?"

"I'm just trying to remember how far we went out here on the couch before we hit the bedroom," he said.

"There's only one way to find out," Max said, laughing as he looked at me. "Full speed ahead, Captain."

"Hang on," Jennifer said, frowning at Max as she got up to fiddle with the connections. The screen went blank, and she quickly clicked through the rest of the photos of her and Naylor on her laptop then reconnected the television to the computer. "We're okay."

"Who was it that spiked your drink at the club?" Max said.

"One of my political opponents," Jennifer said. "Someone you know, and someone who is going to be very surprised and humbled when my book comes out."

"I smell a comeback," Max said, grinning at her.

"You can bet on it," Jennifer said, her eyes dancing. Then she looked at me and motioned for me to continue.

"Nobody has been trying to blackmail either one of you?" I said.

"Absolutely not," Jennifer said.

"Oh, no," Naylor said, a puzzle piece dropping into place. "You think Melinda was blackmailing somebody."

"I do," I said, nodding. "And I think that the person being blackmailed is convinced that you're the one doing it."

"Because they've seen the photos and know they were shot from my loft," Naylor said.

"Yeah," I said. "Melinda had full access to your loft, right?"

"Sure, she had her own access card, but you already know that," he said, frowning at me.

"Yeah, I knew that," I said, my face red with embarrassment. "And her roommate said she spent a couple of nights a week at your place."

"She did," Naylor said. "My place was empty a lot of the time, so I was happy to have her around to keep an eye on things."

"Because you were usually out clubbing with Thomas, right?"

"No, because I was always here," Naylor said, shaking his head at me.

"Sure, sure."

"Try to keep up," Naylor said.

"Hey, there's no need to get snarky," I snapped.

"Oh, I'm sorry. Does the burglar-housekeeper have something to say?" he said, returning my glare.

"Point taken, I said, reaching for the remote. "Moving on."

I quickly advanced through the rest of the pictures of Jennifer and Naylor and landed on a fresh set of photos of a man sitting in a chair facing the window. A naked woman was draped over him, and her bare back displayed a massive tattoo of a coiled snake.

"Cool tattoo," Chef Claire said, staring up at the image.

"Man, that's a lot of needlepoint to sit through," Josie said, frowning. "That had to hurt."

"Absolutely," Chef Claire said.

"That's the guy who was hitting on me at the party," Josie said.

"Jeremiah Walters," Jennifer said.

"Oh, yeah, I remember," I said, grinning at Josie. "He's the guy who tried to lowball you."

"Shut it."

I progressed through the photos that got increasingly graphic, and when I landed on the final one, I grimaced and quickly advanced to a fresh set of photos of the model, Claudine, and her girlfriend, Paradis. While not as explicit as the photos of the woman with the snake tattoo, they were definitely intimate and not anything I'd like floating around.

"Some of those photos are definitely something a blackmailer could use," Max said.

"I can't believe Melinda was trying to blackmail somebody," Naylor said.

"Maybe she needed the money," I said.

"No, that can't be it," Naylor said, shaking his head. "She didn't spend much, and I paid her well. She had plenty of money." Then he rubbed his forehead. "But I suppose she could have decided she needed more."

I pressed the remote, and a photo of Victor Rollins and Wilma appeared. I worked my way through the series, and most of them showed the two of them relaxing in their living room, reading, or talking and laughing. But in a couple of the shots, they were obviously angry with each other.

"Nothing there," Naylor said, motioning for me to continue.

I spent the next ten minutes clicking through the rest of the photos. Several other individuals and couples were featured in various locations around the city, but there was nothing in any of them that seemed damaging enough to force someone to pay money to stop them from being published.

"That's all of them," I said, tossing the remote on the table. I glanced around the room. "What do you think?"

"I think they'd make one heck of a book," Jennifer said.

"Melinda couldn't have been going after Claudine and Paradis," Naylor said, concentrating hard. "They'd both love the publicity."

"Then it has to be Jeremiah," Jennifer said. "But he's such a player, he might enjoy the attention."

"Is he married?" I said.

"No. And I see different women with him all the time," Jennifer said.

"Maybe the woman with the tattoo is married," I said.

"And maybe the wife of someone he works with," Max said.

"That's a distinct possibility," Jennifer said. "It's too bad we couldn't see her face in any of the photos."

"Yeah, but that tattoo has to be pretty unique," I said. "And she's obviously in good shape."

"What does that have to do with anything?" Josie said, frowning.

"I'm pretty sure she works out a lot," I said, then looked at Jennifer. "Do you have a gym in the building?"

"We do," Jennifer said. "A nice gym. And a pool and sauna."

"If she lives here and works out, somebody would have noticed that tattoo," I said.

"I can't imagine who she might be," Jennifer said. "My guess is that she doesn't live here."

"Maybe we could check out tattoo parlors in the area," I said. "You know if we don't get lucky with the gym thing."

"Your plan is to hang out in a gym?" Josie said.

"Why not? I'm sure I can figure out a way to remain inconspicuous."

"Sure," Josie said, grinning. "You hanging out at the gym. Nothing suspicious about that."

Chapter 20

I tiptoed my way along the unshoveled sidewalk and climbed the short set of steps. I tucked the bag I was holding under my arm and pressed the doorbell. Moments later, a disheveled Shirley opened the door. She was wearing a bathrobe over her pajamas, and if she felt anything like she looked, she had my deepest sympathies.

"Hey," Shirley said, coughing.

"How are you doing?" I said, holding out the bag. "I brought you some soup."

"Thanks. That was sweet of you," she said, taking the bag. "Come on in."

"Are you guys contagious?" I said, staying right where I was in the doorway.

"I don't think so. The worst is over," she said, turning around and shuffling back into the living room where I heard a TV blaring the news.

I entered the house and closed the door behind me. Shirley set the bag on the coffee table and plopped back down on a couch next to Bill who was also in pajamas with a blanket wrapped around him. He glanced over his shoulder at me and managed a small nod.

"Hey, Suzy," he said, then blew his nose.

Shirley frowned at the handful of tissues in Bill's hand then held out a small wastebasket close to him. He tossed them in then sank back into the couch, apparently worn out from the effort.

"Have a seat," Shirley said, turning the TV off and pointing at a nearby chair.

"I think I'll just sit over there if that's okay with you," I said. "Not that it's going to make a lot of difference." I sniffed the air. "What's that smell?"

"Menthol, lemon, and bourbon," Bill said, sipping from a steaming mug.

"And germs," Shirley said, coughing.

"Yeah. And lots of germs," Bill said.

"Man, I hate to say it, but you guys look awful," I said, crossing my fingers and toes and praying I didn't catch whatever they had.

"Actually, we're doing a lot better today," Shirley said.

"Yeah, I'm feeling downright peachy," Bill said, setting his mug down to blow his nose again. "What did you need to see us about?"

I reached into my bag, removed Melinda's journal and the storage device filled with photos and handed them over. Shirley took a quick look at the storage device then tossed it on the table. She began flipping through the journal as Bill glanced over her shoulder.

"Okay, this is the journal you mentioned on the phone yesterday," Shirley said, looking up. "Since my vision is a bit blurry, you want to give us the short version?"

Starting with my conversation with Melinda's roommate, I gave them an overview of the previous day's events and hit the high points, ending with a recap of last night's dinner at Jennifer's. As they listened, they both leaned forward on the couch, their heads propped up in their hands and elbows resting on their knees. When I finally stopped talking, they sank back into the couch, exhausted.

"So, the girl was the blackmailer," Bill said to the ceiling.

"It certainly looks like it," I said.

"But the person being blackmailed was convinced it was Naylor," Shirley said, sipping her hot toddy.

"Yeah," I said, frowning at something Bill had hacked up and was examining in the light. He took one final look at the tissue then tossed it into the trash. "That's disgusting." He shrugged at me and sank back into the couch. I glanced at Shirley. "Between Naylor's reputation and the fact that the photos were shot from his loft, it was a logical assumption."

"And whoever tried to kill Naylor actually ended up killing the right person?" Bill said to the ceiling then glanced back and forth at us. "You know, the right person as far as the person who was being blackmailed wanted dead." He frowned. "I'm babbling."

"No, I got it, sweetie," Shirley said, patting his leg. "But you might want to go easy with the bourbon in your toddies." She refocused on me. "Naylor is involved with Jennifer Bell?"

"Yeah, they're in love," I said.

"I didn't see that one coming," Shirley said, then began to cough long and loud. "And he spent the night before the murder at her place?" She pointed at the end table next to my chair. "Toss me that box of tissues, please."

"He did," I said, throwing her the box.

"Naylor's sure Melinda didn't stay at his place that night?" Shirley said.

"Yeah, he's positive," I said. "He remembers Melinda telling him she had dinner plans and then was heading home to meet her roommate for drinks."

"And the roommate confirmed they had a couple of drinks that night, then went home and were there all night," Bill said.

"That's right," Shirley said, nodding. "She did say that. Did Naylor say what time he left his place for good that day?"

"It was around six. He dropped off some dry cleaning, went to the grocery store, then headed straight to Jennifer's loft. He didn't leave until nine the next morning to head home and get ready for the photo shoot with the dogs."

"So, whoever sprinkled the poison on Naylor's pillows had about a fifteen-hour window?"

"Yeah, that sounds about right," I said. "Plenty of time. But why didn't the blackmailer take Naylor's camera and computer when they put the powder on the pillows?"

"Maybe he kept them locked them up at night," Bill said.

"Or maybe he took them with him to Jennifer's place to do some work," Shirley said, shrugging.

"Yeah, I guess that makes sense," I said, frowning. "You want to take a look at the photos?"

"Maybe in a bit," Bill said, coughing. "At the moment, I think I need a nap."

"Yeah, me too," Shirley said, then glanced at me. "You said you wanted us to take a good look at Jeremiah Walters and some woman with a snake tattoo?"

"They seem to be the most logical suspects at the moment," I said, nodding. "The photos of Claudine and Paradis are also pretty revealing, but Naylor is convinced they'd be more than happy if they got published."

"You got photos of Paradis?" Bill said, sitting up on the couch suddenly wide awake.

"I thought you wanted to take a nap," Shirley said with a laugh that transitioned into a coughing spell.

"Well, when duty calls, right?" he said. "What sort of photos are they?"

"What?" I said, frowning.

"You know, are they doing the model thing and posing for the camera?"

210

"No, Melinda managed to catch them in some of their more tender moments. They're more like action shots."

"Action shots? Really?"

"Yes, but *tasteful* action shots."

"Settle down," Shirley said, laughing and shaking her head at her fiancé. "You're gonna have a relapse." She blew her nose, tossed the tissues in the trash, then looked at me. "You figured all this out in one day?"

"Yeah, I guess I did," I said, chuffed.

Shirley glanced over at Bill.

"We should get sick more often."

Chapter 21

The manager of Jennifer's building was a woman named
Marie who was a very pretty French Canadian in her late
twenties, impeccably dressed, and incredibly snooty. More
accurately, she'd copped her superior attitude as soon as she got
a look at me strolling across the lobby in my parka, jeans, and
work boots. She reluctantly accepted my handshake and stared at
me. Apparently, I was supposed to speak first.

"I'm Suzy Chandler," I said, smiling at her. "I called
earlier."

"Yes, you did," she said, eyeing my outfit with a deep
frown. "From your job at the construction site, I would imagine."

"Good one," I said, flashing her a quick two thumbs up.
"You and Josie would get along great." I gave her outfit an
admiring look. "That's a beautiful dress," I said, nodding.
"Hermes, right?"

She flinched, stunned that I had the faintest clue about
fashion.

"Yes, it is," Marie said, then whispered in French. "La
vache connaît sa mode."

"Oui," I said, giving her a tight-lipped smile. "The cow does
know her fashion. Et la vache sait comment frapper fort."

My retort that the cow also knows how to kick hard caught her by surprise, and she glanced down at my boots before resuming eye contact.

"Yes, I'm sure you do," she said. "I apologize. That was rude of me."

"Don't worry about it," I said, shrugging. "I get that all the time."

"You said over the phone that you might be interested in purchasing one of our lofts?" she said, again all business.

"Yes, I had dinner in one of them last night and was very impressed," I said. "But I'll need to get a good look at the building amenities before I can go any further."

"Of course. I'll be happy to give you a tour," she said, gesturing for me to follow her. "Do you have an idea of how much you'd like to spend? We have three for sale at the moment."

"Not really," I said, walking next to her down a long stretch of what looked like polished teak. "I guess I'll just know it when I see it."

"We also work closely with several local banks if you'd like some assistance with financing," she said, nodding at one of the maintenance staff who passed us going the other way.

"No, I'd just you write a check," I said, glancing around, impressed with both the decor and layout.

"Really?" Marie said, again giving me the once-over.

"Sure," I said, nodding. "Why pay interest on borrowed money I already have, right?"

"Can I ask you what you do for a living?" she said, confused.

"I run a dog inn," I said.

"A doginn?" she said, frowning at me. "What the hell is a doginn?"

"No, a dog…inn."

"I see. And there's money in running a dog inn?"

"Oh, God, no," I said, shaking my head.

"How many dogs do you have?"

"Around sixty at the moment," I said.

"Sixty? I should probably let you know that we have a fairly strict policy on pets," Marie said. "You wouldn't be planning on bringing your dogs with you, right?"

"No, they're really not loft kind of dogs."

"A dog inn," she said, apparently having a hard time wrapping her head around the idea.

"And we've got a couple of restaurants," I said. "Oh, and I almost forgot. We're starting a dog toy business as well."

She looked over at me like I was from another planet, then stopped in front of a metal door and pulled it open.

"Let's start with a look at our pool area," she said, gesturing for me to go first.

I stepped inside the large area that had been designed with a tropical look. A large swimming pool surrounded by lush palms and other flora dominated the space, and I noticed three large hot tubs in different corners of the room. A large wooden sauna occupied the remaining corner. Impressed again, I nodded at my tour guide.

"It's nice, isn't it?" Marie said, looking around the space.

"It's incredible."

If I actually had been looking to buy a place in Ottawa, this certainly wouldn't be a bad option.

"That's our dry sauna," Marie said. "And we have a wet one just on the other side of that wall near the showers."

"Very nice," I said, following her as she walked around the perimeter of the pool.

"Let me show you the gym," she said. "I imagine you're interested in seeing what sort of exercise equipment we offer."

"Sure, sure."

She opened another door and again gestured for me to go in just as her phone rang. She checked the number and frowned.

"I'm so sorry," she said. "But I need to take this call."

"No problem," I said, glancing around the spacious gym. "I'm fine. Take all the time you need."

"I'll meet you inside as soon as I can," she said, answering the call. "I told you we'd talk about it later," she snapped, then glanced at me embarrassed by her outburst. She strolled a safe distance away.

I stepped inside, heard the door click shut behind me and flinched at the fresh memory, then looked around. It had been a while since I'd been in a gym, and I didn't recognize many of the exercise machines. But I did recognize Claudine and Paradis. They were wearing skintight spandex, and both had their hair tied back in a ponytail. They were on stationary bikes and peddling frantically as if trying to escape the stalking paparazzi, but not moving an inch. Sweat was pouring off them, and I got tired just watching them. A few minutes later, they came to a stop, checked some sort of readout on their bikes, then hopped down and began to towel off. They both drank greedily from water bottles, then Paradis noticed me and gave me a small wave.

"Hi," I said, walking toward them.

"Don't tell me," Claudine said, frowning as she tried to remember who I was. "Suzy, right? From the Christmas party."

"That's me," I said, grinning back and forth at them. "That's quite a workout you guys are doing."

"How else would we stay so thin?" Paradis said, taking another long swig of water.

"I don't know," I mumbled with a shrug. "Cigarettes and amphetamines?"

"What?" Paradis said, frowning.

"Nothing," I said, beaming at them. "This is a really nice gym."

"We like it," Claudine said. "There's no riff-raff to deal with."

"Yeah, riff-raff at the gym is the worst," I said.

"We should get going," Paradis said, glancing at her watch.

"That's right," Claudine said. "Our appointment is at two." She glanced at me. "We're getting matching tattoos this afternoon."

"Nice," I said, glancing at Paradis. "Are you going to get another butterfly?"

"How do you know I have a butterfly tattoo?" the supermodel said, glaring at me.

I bit my bottom lip. It had been impossible to miss it last night when we were looking at their photos, but I decided it probably wasn't a good idea to share that bit of news.

"Uh, I think I read about it in Cosmo," I said, my face flushed red.

"How does Cosmo know that?" Paradis said, glancing at Claudine. "Did you say something?"

"I did not."

"Then how did it get out?"

"Who knows?" Claudine said, shrugging. "Who cares? It'll enhance your image as a free spirit. Let's get going. Nice seeing you, Suzy."

"Yeah, take care," I said. "And be careful walking the runway in those heels they make you wear. You could snap an ankle."

I thought it was a solid safety tip, but they both stared blankly at me then headed off with their towels draped over their

217

shoulders. I glanced around the gym and rocked back and forth on my heels as I silently counted to five.

Since I was here, I might as well get a little workout in.

I noticed a man on a treadmill in the far corner of the gym. From the back, it took me a minute to recognize him, then I realized it was George Theo, the mining magnate and current fiancé of the infamous Black Widow. I walked over to the treadmill and stopped in front of him. He was clad head to toe in a black sweat suit that appeared to be leaking into his running shoes. What was left of his hair was soaked with sweat and plastered like a spider web on top of his head.

"Hi, George," I said.

"Hey," he said, uncertain at first who I was. Then he nodded. "Yeah, now I got it. We met at the Christmas party. You're the Dog Girl. Suzy, right?"

"That's me," I said, then noticed he'd turned the treadmill off and coasted to a gentle stop. "You don't need to stop because of me."

"Are you kidding?" he said, breathing heavily. "I've spent the last ten minutes looking for an excuse to stop."

"Let me guess," I said. "You're trying to get in shape for the wedding."

"Guess again," he said with a snort.

"Charlotte's trying to get you into shape before the wedding."

218

"Bingo," he said, reaching for his towel. "You'd think after five marriages, that would be the least of her worries."

"I hate working out," I said.

"You and me both."

"But you're going to be working out all the time on your honeymoon in the Caribbean, right?"

"That's kind of a personal question, wouldn't you say?" he said, grinning at me.

"No, I didn't mean that," I said, embarrassed. "I meant working out snorkeling, swimming, and stuff like that."

"I'll be doing the least amount of those things I can get away with," he said.

"Really?"

"Yeah, I hate the water," he said. "I'm more of a dirt guy."

"Then why did you agree to spend your honeymoon on a boat?" I said.

"I have my reasons," he said, grinning.

"Got it," I said, nodding. "She is a beautiful woman."

"Yes, she is," George said. "And she certainly keeps me on my toes."

"For your sake, I certainly hope so," I whispered.

"What?" he said, staring at me.

"Nothing," I said, shaking my head. But I found it impossible to ignore the look he was giving me. "I'm sorry. It's really none of my business."

"No, it's not," he said, grabbing his bag and removing a metal flask. "But go ahead. What's on your mind?"

"I really shouldn't say anything," I said.

He glanced around, slowly raised his arm and took a long, elaborate swig from the flask. He offered it to me. "Want a hit? Johnny Walker Blue."

"Thanks, but I'll pass," I said, shaking my head.

He repeated the strange arm movement and took another long drink, caught his breath as his eyes watered, then took a third.

"Whew. Okay, that's my set of arm curls," he said, tossing the flask back in his bag. "So, what's on your mind, Suzy?"

"It's just that I've heard a few things about Charlotte's past."

"You mean her five dead ex-husbands?"

"Yeah," I said. "That did sort of grab my attention."

"And you're wondering why I'd be willing to sign up to be number six?" he said, raising an eyebrow.

"Nothing gets past you," I said, laughing.

"Yeah, a lot of people are wondering about that," he said, nodding. "But like I said, I have my reasons. So, what are you doing here?"

"I'm getting a tour of the place," I said.

"You thinking about buying a loft?"

"Maybe. I'm just looking at the moment."

"Well, if you hold off for a while, maybe one of them will suddenly come on the market, right?"

"Oh, let's hope not, George," I said. "But I must say that you don't seem very worried."

"I've spent most of my life blowing the tops off mountains and digging enormous holes in the ground," he said, turning serious. "Not to mention dealing with armies of tree huggers. Don't worry, I can take care of myself."

"I believe you."

"Suzy, I'm so sorry to keep you waiting," Marie called out as she entered and walked briskly across the gym.

"Don't worry about it," I said. "I'm having a great time talking with Mr. Theo."

"Hello, George," Maria said. "How are you doing today?"

"I'm great," he said. "I just finished my power walk and a set of arm curls." He winked at me. "I have a couple more sets of curls to do, but I think I'll do them upstairs in the loft."

"Don't overdo it, George," I said, grinning at him.

"I won't," he said. "But I should probably call my buddy Johnny Blue and have him help me out."

"Good plan."

"Ladies, have a wonderful day," he said, giving us a small salute and heading off.

"He's a nice man," I said, watching him depart.

"Yes, he is," Marie said, also staring after him. "And that's what has us all very worried."

"I think I've seen all I need to," I said.

"What do you think?"

"The place is amazing," I said. "But I have a few others to check out before I make a decision. Can I get back to you?"

"Of course," Marie said. "You know where to find me."

I followed her out a different door that led back to the teak hallway we'd used on our way in. Halfway down the hall, I saw Wilma heading toward us. She was wearing her workout clothes and had a towel draped over her shoulders.

"Suzy," she said, coming to a stop. "What are you doing here?"

"Hey, Wilma," I said, giving her a quick hug. "Marie was just giving me a tour."

"Suzy is thinking about buying in," Marie said.

"Oh, that would be great," Wilma said. "Are Claudine and Paradis still in there? I was supposed to work out with them, but I'm running very late."

"No, they were there, spandex blazing," I said. "But they said they had to get to an appointment. Apparently, they're getting matching tattoos."

"Really?" Wilma said, tugging at the baggy sweatshirt she was wearing. "What a stupid thing to do."

"I take it you're not a tattoo fan?" I said.

"I think it's the dumbest decision anyone could ever make," Wilma said.

"I have a tattoo," Marie said softly. "I like it."

My neurons flared, and I stared at her. I decided to do a little fishing.

"I've always wondered if it hurts? It has to hurt, right?" I said.

"Absolutely," Wilma said, nodding. "There's no way around it, right?"

"Well, having a needle going in and out of my back certainly wasn't the most enjoyable experience I've ever had," Marie said. "But in the end, it was worth it."

"Your back?" I said to Marie. "Ouch, right?"

"That would be the word for it," Wilma said, shaking her head. "I'll see you guys later. Say hi to everyone for me."

We watched her head inside the gym then continued toward the front door.

"My boyfriend loves the tattoo," Marie said. "And he wants me to get another one. I'm thinking about getting a butterfly, but I can't decide where to put it."

I flashed back to the photos of Paradis and grimaced. I glanced back at her.

"Choose wisely."

Chapter 22

I leaned forward to refill everyone's wine glass then sat
back down in my chair. Then I leaned to my right and gave Max
a kiss on the cheek before focusing on my dinner, a crockpot
stew Chef Claire had put together that morning before she and
Max and the dogs had gone cross-country skiing. It was the third
day in a row for her, and she looked worn out. But not as worn
out as the dogs who had stretched out in front of the fire as soon
as they'd gotten home and hadn't moved since. Chef Claire
reached for a piece of garlic bread and winced.

"Sore?" Josie deadpanned.

"You know I'm sore," Chef Claire said.

"Yeah, but I like hearing it from you," she said, grinning.

"Shut it."

"I can't believe you went out there three days in a row," I
said, shaking my head. I took a sip of wine. "People are going to
start questioning your sanity." I glanced at Max. "And I'm
getting a little worried about yours, too."

"It's great exercise," Max said, squeezing my thigh.

"Yes, it is," Chef Claire said. "You should try it."

Josie laughed way too long and hard.

"Hey, for the record, I was at the gym earlier today," I said.

All three of them paused mid-bite to stare at me.

"You were at the gym?" Chef Claire said.

"Yes."

"Doing what?" Josie said.

"Well, let's see. I was at the stationary bike *and* the treadmill."

"Really?" Josie said, confused.

"Yes," I said. "And I was also thinking about doing some arm curls, but I decided it was too early in the day."

"I'm impressed," Max said, leaning close and giving my thigh another gentle squeeze. "You should sleep well tonight."

"I'm sure I will," I said, nuzzling his neck.

"Hey, I'm trying to eat here," Josie deadpanned. "Oh, I almost forgot. John Naylor called earlier and said he had a cancellation. He can reshoot the dogs the day after tomorrow."

"We need to spend two more days here?" I said, making a face. "Not the briar patch."

"Yeah, I thought that would break your heart," Josie said. "Since we're here, we might as well get it done, right?"

"Have you talked with Sammy and Jill?"

"I did," Josie said. "Everything's fine at the Inn."

"And things are very quiet at the restaurant," Chef Claire said. "So, I'm good."

"You don't mind?" I said to Max.

"I'm sure I'll be able to deal with it," he said, laughing. "But you might have to go skiing on your own, Chef Claire. I don't think I can handle another day out there."

"That's okay," she said, arching her back. "I've had my fill."

"What gym did you go to?" Max said.

"I was at the one in Jennifer's building. I took a break from my tour," I said, reaching for a piece of garlic bread.

"Oh, that's right," Max said. "The search for the tattooed lady. How did you do?"

"A total whiff," I said, shaking my head. "But I did run into the two models and George Theo." I grinned at Josie. "Paradis sends her love."

"Good for Paradis," Josie said, making a face at me.

"And on my way out, I ran into Wilma. She said to say hi."

"How did you manage to get a tour?" Max said, pushing his plate away and sitting back in his chair.

"I told the building manager I was thinking about buying a loft," I said.

"That's all you'd need, right?" Josie said. "One more thing to worry about."

"Yeah," I said, nodding.

"Not to mention the size of the mortgage on a place like that," Max said, taking a sip of wine.

"No, if I was going to buy it, I'd just write a check," I said, casually waving it off as my neurons began to flare.

"What?" Max said, staring at me.

"What?" I said, staring back at him, then glancing down. "What is it? Did I spill something?"

"You said you'd just write a check for it," Max said.

"Yeah, I guess I did say that," I whispered, then glanced at back and forth at Josie and Chef Claire.

Max continued to stare at me as I toyed with what was left on my plate.

"I think somebody decided not to tell somebody something," Josie said to Chef Claire.

"I think you're right," Chef Claire said. "Should we leave the table?"

"No, you're fine," I said, exhaling.

"Tell me what?" Max said, confused.

"I didn't tell you about my money," I said after a long pause.

"You have money?"

"Yeah, a little," I said, shrugging.

Josie and Chef Claire snorted. I shot them a dirty look, and they both sipped their wine in silence.

"Why didn't you say something?" Max said.

"I don't like to talk about it."

"Okay, I can understand that," he said, nodding. "You were worried I might only be interested in your money."

"Not really," I said. "My not talking about it is sort of a defense mechanism."

"You must know by now that I wouldn't care if you were dead broke, right?"

"I do," I said, placing my hand over his. "I probably should have said something by now. I'm sorry."

"No, don't apologize," Max said. "It's certainly not a problem. I'm just surprised. And more than a little intrigued. What sort of money are we talking about?"

I leaned over and whispered the number in his ear. He flinched and stared at me, then glanced back and forth at Josie and Chef Claire who both slowly nodded their heads.

"You're joking, right?" he said.

"No," I said softly. "Not only do I not like to talk about it, I never joke about it. It's a ridiculous number."

"Well, now I understand why you'd just write a check for the loft," he said, shaking his head in amazement. "And it would certainly be a lot faster than your usual real estate deal. You know, just write the check and walk out with the deed."

My neurons exploded, and I flinched in my chair and grabbed my forehead. I focused on my breathing as I waited it out staring off into the distance.

"Uh-oh," Josie said. "Here we go again."

"Are you okay?" Max said.

"She'll be fine," Chef Claire said, casually sipping her wine. "Just give her a minute."

"She looks like she's seen a ghost," Max said, patting my hand. "Hey, where are you?"

"I'm fine," I whispered. I sat quietly and waited for my neurons to coalesce. Eventually, I focused on my immediate surroundings and smiled at Max. "Excuse me for a minute. I need to make a phone call."

"Who are you calling?" Max said.

"I've got a real estate question I need to run by somebody," I said, then looked at Josie. "Can I borrow your phone?"

"Sure," she said, reaching into her bag and handing it over.

"I'll be right back," I said, heading into the living room. I bent down to pet all four of the sleeping dogs who thumped their tails but continued to snore softly in front of the fire. I located the number on Josie's phone and made the call.

"Hi, Josie. What's up?"

"No, it's me. How are you doing, Paulie?"

"Hey, Suzy. How's Ottawa?"

"It's great. Am I interrupting anything?"

Paulie put his phone on speaker.

"She wants to know if she's interrupting," Paulie said, laughing.

"Hello, darling," my mother said. "Your timing is impeccable."

"Sorry, Mom. But I have a question for Paulie."

"Shoot," Paulie said.

"You used to be a criminal, right?"

"That's your question?" Paulie said.

"No, that's not my question," I said, frowning. "I was just establishing the framework for the conversation."

"Darling, must you?" my mother said. "What on earth does Paulie's past have to do with anything? What do you need? We're completely snowed in, and we were just about to have dessert. If you catch my drift."

"Got it, Mom," I said, frowning. "I've got a real estate question."

"She could have given me a thousand guesses, and I wouldn't have come up with that," I heard my mother whisper.

"I'm not much of a real estate expert," Paulie said, laughing. "But I'll give it a shot."

"When you were working on the dark side, you must have come in contact with people who dealt with real estate transactions that were a bit out of the ordinary, right?"

"If you mean out of the ordinary deals that didn't go through traditional lending practices, sure. All the time," he said.

"And you did things on both sides of the border, right?" I said, rubbing my forehead.

"If you're asking me if my former business occasionally took me into Canada, yes, it did."

"Ottawa?"

"Sure," Paulie said. "It's the capital city, and a lot of deals come out of there. I've always preferred Montreal, but Ottawa's a nice place."

"If I wanted to do a real estate deal in a hurry, who would I talk to about that?"

"Darling, if you're thinking about buying a place up there, just write them a check."

"Thanks, Mom. I'll do that," I said, shaking my head. "But, hypothetically, who would I want to talk to, Paulie?"

"I'm assuming you'd want to keep it as quiet as you could, close the deal in a hurry, and make sure the deal was in cash, right?"

"You're good," I said, laughing. "That's exactly what I'd want to do."

"Well, if I were looking to do something like that up there, there's only one guy I'd use," Paulie said.

"Who's that?" I said, squinting as my headache deepened.

"Morty the Milker."

"Didn't you ever work with anybody who had a normal name?" I said, frowning. "What is it with you guys?"

"It's the perfect nickname for him," Paulie said. "Morty knows that pretty much everybody who comes to him for help must be desperate. And as such, he likes to squeeze people pretty hard. Hence, The Milker."

"Is he still in business?"

"I'm sure he is," Paulie said. "Morty will keep working until he drops. He loves what he does."

"Squeezing desperate people?"

"Yeah," Paulie said. "And making money in the process, of course."

"I need to meet him," I said.

"Why?" my mother said.

"I just have some questions for him."

"Again, why?"

"I'm just trying to figure something out, Mom."

"Please don't tell me you're sticking your nose into the investigation," she said.

I remained silent for several moments, then my mother continued.

"Darling?"

"What?"

"Aren't you going to answer me?"

"You asked me not to tell you."

"I don't believe it," she snapped. "Just let the police handle it, darling."

"Oh, I'm working with them," I said. "But they have the flu at the moment."

"Well, then that changes everything," my mother said.

"There's no need to get snarky, Mom."

"Is this guy dangerous?" my mother said to Paulie.

"No, Morty's a sweetheart," Paulie said. "But she shouldn't drop in unannounced. Let me give him a call and prepare him for what's about to descend."

"Funny," I said, listening closely to their sidebar conversation. "Thanks for doing that, Paulie. You'll let me know as soon as you talk to him?"

"I will," Paulie said. "I'll give him a call right after we have dessert."

"Please don't anything stupid, darling. Like getting yourself into a dangerous position."

"You either, Mom," I said, grinning.

"You're really not funny, young lady."

Chapter 23

Morty the Milker lived in a large stone house in a high-end section of the city called Old Ottawa South on what looked like a couple of acres. I drove up the long stretch of driveway that had been plowed to perfection and parked in front of the house. I rang the bell, and a woman somewhere in her thirties answered the door and smiled at me.

"Ms. Chandler, right?"

"Please call me Suzy," I said, extending my hand.

"I'm Lucinda Miller," she said, waving me inside. "My father is expecting you. Let me take your coat."

"Thanks," I said, taking a look around as I handed her my parka. "Your home is amazing."

"Oh, I'm just visiting," she said. "But thank you. My father loves it here. Come. He's in the atrium."

I followed her down a long hall then into a large room that was dominated by glass and plants. A small man in his sixties with a full head of gray hair got up from his chair and beamed at me.

"Ms. Chandler, I presume," he said, reaching out for my hand, then surprising me by gently kissing it.

"Suzy," I said, smiling at him. "It's nice to meet you, Mr. Miller. And thanks for seeing me on short notice."

"Any friend of Paulie's is always welcome here," he said, gesturing at the overstuffed chair directly across from his.

"Do you need anything, Father?" Lucinda said. "Perhaps something to drink?"

"Suzy, can we get you anything?" Morty said.

"No, I'm good, thanks."

"We're fine, Lucinda. Thank you."

"I'll leave you two alone then," she said, exiting with a small wave.

"I love it when she visits," he said, staring after her. "I just wish she was here under better circumstances."

I looked at him and waited for him to continue.

"She's going through a divorce," he said.

"I'm sorry to hear that," I said. "They can be nasty."

"Yes, it did start out that way," Morty said, smiling. "But her husband recently made the wise choice to calm down and be a bit more...pliable."

"A decision I assume he needed some help getting to?" I said, cocking my head.

Morty laughed and nodded his head at me.

"Good one. Paulie said you didn't pull any punches."

"Yeah, I really need to start working on that," I said, glancing around the room. "Your home is magnificent."

"Thank you," he said, looking around with pride. "I was able to pick it up several years ago for a song."

"What song was that?"

Again, he laughed and didn't stop until he started coughing.

"You're funny. I think he was singing, *Let Me Go, You're Hurtin' Me*," Morty said.

"I'm not familiar with that one," I said, playing along.

"At least that's what I think he was trying to say at the time," Morty said, laughing. "The man had a terrible singing voice."

"It's probably hard to sing with a foot on your throat, right?" I said, raising an eyebrow at him.

"Yes, I'm sure it is. But, no, it was nothing like that," he said, waving me away with a coy smile. "He just needed to get out in a hurry, and I was able to accommodate him." He wiped his eyes with a tissue and shook his head at me. "You're a piece of work. So, how can I help you?"

"I need to show you a photo of someone," I said, reaching for my bag.

"And you'd like to know if I've done business with this person?" Morty said, leaning forward.

"Yes."

"Can I ask you why you need to know?"

"Because I think it involves a blackmail attempt that turned into murder," I said, handing him the photo.

"Oh, that's dreadful. I hate hearing about things like that" he said, then his eyes narrowed. "I certainly hope you don't think I was somehow involved."

"Absolutely not," I said, shaking my head.

"Okay," Morty said, nodding. He studied the photograph then looked at me. "Yeah, I did that deal a few weeks ago."

"That's all I needed to know, Mr. Miller," I said, getting up. "Thank you very much."

"Don't you want to know how much I paid for it?"

"It was five hundred thousand, right?"

"How on earth did you know that?" he said, frowning up at me.

"Lucky guess."

"If you're in the market," he said, giving me a small smile. "I still have it. Since you're a friend of Paulie, I can let you have it for six."

"Thanks, Mr. Miller," I said, extending my hand. "But I don't know what to do with all the stuff I've already got."

"Yes, having too much stuff around can be a real problem," he said, nodding. "I never know where to put everything."

"Yeah, tell me about it," I said, heading for the door, my head packed to the rafters with my neurons on overload and looking for a place to land.

Chapter 24

I grabbed the ticket from the parking attendant who was bundled tight in a parka and headed inside the restaurant. I stood near the door and waited until my eyes adjusted to the light, then spotted Victor Rollins sitting at a table near the back. I removed my coat as I walked across the dining room and sat down across from him.

"How are you doing?" he said, glancing up from the menu.

"I'm okay," I said softly.

"Are you sure?" he said, staring at me.

"I'm just tired," I said.

"Have you been here before?" he said, again studying the menu.

"No."

"Their soups are fantastic," he said. "I'm glad you called."

"I thought we should talk," I said, rubbing my forehead.

"Sure, and I have an update for you. Abby and I met again yesterday, and things are looking great. Did you get the photo shoot rescheduled?"

"Yeah, for tomorrow," I said. "If we need to do it."

Victor frowned at my comment, then stared at the front door of the restaurant.

"Hey, aren't those the two cops from the Middleton case? The ones you brought to the Christmas party."

"I'm sure it is," I said, not bothering to turn around.

Bill and Shirley approached the table, removed their coats and sat down.

"Well, why don't you just make yourself comfortable?" Victor said, laughing as he glanced back and forth at them.

"We were invited," Bill said, still sounding like he had a bad head cold.

"You were?" Victor said with a frown. Then he looked at me. "What's going on, Suzy?"

"Like I said, I thought we should talk," I said, then looked at the two detectives. "How are you guys feeling?"

"Like crap," Bill said.

"Maybe some soup will help," Shirley said, coughing as she reached for a menu. "I wouldn't wish this thing on my worst enemy."

"Okay, somebody needs to tell me what the heck is going on," Victor said.

I glanced back and forth at Bill and Shirley, and they both gestured for me to take the lead.

"You go ahead," Bill said. "If I try talking, I might throw up."

"We invited you here to talk about Melinda's murder," I said.

"Have you figured out who did it?" Victor said, glancing around the table.

"I'm afraid so," I said, looking at the cops who silently nodded their agreement.

"That's great," Victor said, perking up. "Whoever killed her deserves to go away for a long time."

"Yeah, that's what we think, too," Shirley said, pushing her menu away. "What's that old saying about eating when you're sick?"

"You mean, feed a cold, starve a fever?" I said.

"Yeah, that's the one," Shirley said.

"What about it?"

"What are you supposed to do when you have both?" she said, coughing.

"If it were me, I'd probably just start eating," I said, shrugging.

"Good call," she said, blowing her nose.

"How's Wilma doing?" I said.

"She's okay," Victor said, confused. "She said she ran into you yesterday. Are you really thinking about buying a place in our building?"

"No," I said, shaking my head.

"Suzy," he said. "How about you quit dancing and just tell me what's on your mind?"

"Okay," I said. "How strained is your relationship with Wilma at the moment?"

"What? What sort of question is that?" Victor said, annoyed.

"It's a very important one, Victor."

I lowered my head, then glanced across the table at him and maintained eye contact.

"If you must know, we're going through a rough patch at the moment," Victor said. "But what does that have to do with who killed Melinda?"

We waited out a long silence as Victor kept glancing around the table. Then he sat back in his chair and laughed.

"Please don't tell me you think I killed her," he said. "That's it, isn't it? I don't believe it. I'm having a deja vu moment back to the time when you guys thought I'd killed Middleton. I can't believe you people. You think I killed her."

"No, Victor, we don't," I whispered. "Wilma killed Melinda."

"What? That's ridiculous," he said.

"Has Wilma been cheating on you?" I said.

Victor fell silent and stared off into the distance.

"She has been pretty distant and preoccupied lately," he said. "And I've had my suspicions, but I'm not convinced she's been sleeping around. And Wilma would never do anything to hurt her. She loved Melinda."

"Melinda was very fond of both of you, right?" I said. "You said at the Christmas party that you and Wilma had made her believe that true love was possible."

241

"Yeah, Melinda did like to say that," Victor said.

"But not lately, right?"

"As a matter of fact, no," he said, frowning.

"And Wilma mentioned at the party that she'd recently sold a house. You guys were fighting about it."

"Yeah, she decided to unload the house her parents left her," Victor said. "I thought she was crazy to sell it, but she said she was tired of maintaining it and that it had too many bad memories."

"Do you know how much she sold it for?" I said.

"No, she wouldn't tell me," Victor said. "Wilma's turned very secretive lately. Maybe she is having an affair."

"This is going to sound like a very strange question," I said, forcing a small smile.

"Oh, I'm sorry, I thought you'd already started with the strange questions," Victor said.

Bill and Shirley tried to laugh but ended up fighting off coughing fits.

"Go ahead," Victor said, glaring at me.

"Does Wilma have any tattoos?"

"That's your question?"

"Yeah."

"Well, you're right about it being strange," Victor said. "Yeah, she has a tattoo."

"A giant snake on her back?" I said, reaching for my bag.

"She told you about it?" he said, thoroughly confused. "That'd odd. She usually doesn't like to talk about it since she regrets ever getting it in the first place. What on earth is going on?"

I slid the set of photos of the tattooed woman wrapped around Jeremiah Walters across the table. Victor slowly flipped through them, then tapped the edges until they were in a neat stack and slid them back to me.

"I can't believe she's sleeping with that creep," Victor said, exhaling loudly. "Okay, she's having an affair. But that doesn't mean she killed Melinda."

I slid the photos back to him.

"Look closely at the photos, Victor, and tell me what you see," I said.

"I don't need to see them again, Suzy. It's pretty clear what they're doing."

"No, take a look at them from the point of view of the person taking the photos," I said, glancing up as our server approached.

The server did a quick U-turn when he saw Bill waving him away. Victor studied the photos then nodded.

"They were shot from Naylor's loft, weren't they?"

"Yes, they were," I said.

"I can't believe the crap that pervert does," Victor said, glancing at Bill and Shirley. "Isn't there some way you can arrest the guy for invading people's privacy like that?"

"I'm sure we could," Shirley said. "If he'd been the one who took the photos."

"What are you talking about? If he didn't take…Melinda? She took them?"

All three of us nodded in silence.

"But why would she do something like that?" Victor said.

"We're pretty sure, at first, she was just trying to get some shots she could use in her book," Shirley said.

"She mentioned something about wanting to do a book," Victor said. "She was spying on people from Naylor's place?"

"Yeah," I said.

"But Naylor wasn't involved?"

"No, he wasn't," I said. "The night before Melinda was killed, she had dinner at your place, didn't she?"

Victor thought for a moment, then nodded.

"She did," Victor said. "It was a strange night. Wilma and Melinda were both in a weird mood."

"And Wilma ducked out for a while at some point during the evening," I said.

"Yeah, she ran out to the store to pick something up," Victor said. "How on earth did you know that?"

"Because that was when she somehow managed to get hold of Melinda's access card to Naylor's place," I said. "And she went over there to put the poisoned powder in Naylor's bedroom."

"Why would she do that?" Victor said.

"Because she was convinced that it was Naylor who was trying to blackmail her," Bill said.

"Blackmail?" Victor said.

"Yeah, I imagine that Wilma received a copy of those photos in the mail, figured out where they'd been taken and logically assumed Naylor was the one trying to squeeze her."

"Melinda was blackmailing Wilma?" Victor said, devastated. "But why?"

"Because Wilma had disappointed her," I said. "I imagine Melinda was crushed when she found out what Wilma was doing behind your back."

"That's nuts," Victor said, shaking his head.

"To us, yeah, I guess it is," Shirley said. "But to someone as fragile as Melinda was it probably didn't seem that crazy at all. Intense anger and disappointment that turned into the need for revenge. We've seen stranger things."

"Do you have any proof?" Victor said.

"We could probably make a case," Shirley said. "But we'd like to have something more tangible."

"And that's why I called and invited you to lunch," I said. "We need your help."

"Doing what?"

"You need to lend Wilma some money," I said.

"Can I ask why?"

"Because she's going to get a phone call later today from somebody demanding another payment."

"How much am I supposed to lend her?"

"Five hundred thousand," I said, again reaching into my bag.

"What?" he said, frowning. "Why five hundred grand?"

I slid a copy of Melinda's Life in Moments poem across the table.

"Because Melinda decided that the first five hundred notes weren't enough," I said.

Victor read then reread the poem. Eventually, he slid it back across the table.

"The reference to the five hundred notes not being enough means that Wilma's already paid half a million?" Victor said, rereading the poem.

"Yes, we're pretty sure that's what it means," Shirley said, then coughed and blew her nose again.

"She used the proceeds from the sale of her house," Victor said.

"We're also pretty sure about that," Shirley said.

"No wonder she was in such a hurry to unload it. My girlfriend is a murderer?" Victor said, staring down at the table. "And she ended up killing Melinda by mistake. No wonder Wilma's been off the planet since she died. Wilma still thinks Naylor is the blackmailer, doesn't she?" Victor said.

"I'm sure she does," I said. "That's why we need your help before she decides to take another run at him."

"Wow," he said after a long silence. "I sure know how to pick 'em." He took a deep breath and exhaled loudly. "I probably could have eventually gotten past an affair. But murder is something else altogether. Okay, I'll play. I'll go to the bank right after lunch." He glanced at the detectives. "Withdrawing five hundred grand in cash is going to raise a lot of questions."

"We'll come with you and explain it to the bank manager," Shirley said.

"Okay," Victor said, resigned. "Is that it?"

"There's just one more thing," I said.

"What's that?"

"Do you know if Wilma has a safe deposit box there?"

"As a matter of fact, she does."

"Then would you mind taking the key along when you go to the bank?" I said.

"Why?"

"Because I think you might have my phone."

Chapter 25

I arrived at John Naylor's loft around six-thirty the next evening carrying two plastic bags filled with Greek takeout. Just because we were about to confront Wilma didn't mean we had to do it on an empty stomach. I hung my coat on a hook and handed the bags to Naylor who headed for the kitchen then organized the boxes in a row on the counter. Bill and Shirley both stared at the contents of the boxes with interest.

"It looks like you've got your appetite back," I said, watching Bill fill his plate.

"It's nice to feel human again," he said, biting a Dolmades in half. "What did Wilma say when you called back to confirm the meeting?"

"She said she had the money and would be here at seven," Naylor said, his nervousness apparent to all of us.

"Good job," Bill said, reaching for another stuffed grape leaf.

"You're sure this is the best place to do it?" Naylor said, wringing his hands as he glanced around the loft.

"Yeah," Shirley said. "Once she's up here, we'll be bringing in a dozen cops to keep an eye on the elevators and all the exits. She's not going anywhere." Shirley said. "Besides, it's too freaking cold to do the exchange outside."

Bill snorted and shook his head, then focused on his Pastitsio, a Greek lasagna with a béchamel sauce and minced lamb filling.

"Too cold?" John Naylor said to Shirley. "You're a Canadian cop. And it's November. What do you do in February?"

"Usually pray that I die in a warm bed," Shirley said, reaching for a Dolmades. "Just because I live with winter doesn't mean I have to like it."

"She's such a baby," Bill said, laughing as he popped an olive into his mouth.

"How can you guys be so casual about all this?" Naylor said, glancing back and forth at them.

"We've had lots of practice," Bill said, shrugging.

"There's a woman about to show up here who thinks I'm blackmailing her," Naylor said, his voice rising a notch. "Not to mention the fact that she's already tried to kill me."

"Just stick to the script we've worked out, and you'll be fine," Bill said, wiping his mouth. "And we'll be right here with you."

"In my office, right?" I said.

"Yeah," Bill said. "It's close to the living room, and we'll be able to hear a lot better."

"What if she's carrying a gun?" Naylor said.

"I doubt if she'll have a gun," Bill said.

"Gee, thanks, Detective. That makes me feel so much better."

"I suppose you could frisk her when she comes in," Shirley said. "That's probably something she might expect you to do."

"I've never frisked anybody before," Naylor said.

"It's easy," Shirley said. "Come here. I'll show you. Suzy, if you wouldn't mind?"

"Mind what?" I said, frowning through a mouthful of Pastitsio.

"Getting frisked," Shirley said, laughing.

"I'd rather wait until I get back to Max's place if it's all right with you," I said.

"Who's being a baby now?" Bill said, grinning.

Naylor walked over next to me and waited for instructions.

"Stand behind her, John," Shirley said. "Now, when Wilma gets here, have her take her coat off, put the money on the floor, and tell her to raise her hands." Shirley demonstrated, and I followed along. "Great. Just keep them in the air. John, start the frisk from the shoulders and work your way down to her waist patting her along the way."

"How hard do I pat her?" Naylor said.

"Just hard enough to make sure she isn't hiding anything on her body. You'll know," Shirley said.

Naylor began to work his way down my shoulders then he stopped.

"How do I handle her breasts?" Naylor said, embarrassed.

"You don't, John," I said, glaring at Shirley. "Wipe that smirk off your face."

"Sorry," Shirley said, doing her best not to laugh. "Just stay on the outside of them and keep working your way down until you reach her waist."

"Thank you," I said, nodding.

"We'll deal with the breasts when you do the front," Shirley deadpanned.

"Like hell, you will," I snapped.

"I'm joking," Shirley said as she watched Naylor continue. "Good job. Now, kneel down and start working up from her feet. There you go."

I grimaced as I felt Naylor's hands work their way up my legs. When he reached my upper thigh, I flinched and glanced over my shoulder.

"John?"

"Yeah?"

"Do you really think I'd be able to hide a weapon there?"

"Uh, no, probably not," he said, removing his hands.

Bill and Shirley both laughed and I shot them a dirty look.

"Sorry," Naylor said.

"Forget it," I said.

"That's probably not going to happen, but I'll give it a shot," Naylor said, stifling a laugh of his own.

"Okay, let's do the front," Shirley said, clapping her hands together.

"I think he's got it figured out," I said, lowering my arms.

"Is all this really necessary?" Naylor said to the detectives. "Can't you just arrest her when she shows up with the money?"

"We could," Bill said. "But we'd rather get her on tape confessing. Without that, she could just say that you've been blackmailing her, and she was scared about what might happen if she didn't pay up. You know, since you'd already killed Melinda."

"I didn't kill Melinda," Naylor said, scowling at him.

"We know that," Shirley said. "But she was killed here, and you spent a lot of time together. With the right lawyer, a jury might be convinced that you were the one behind both the blackmail and the murder."

"And you have to admit that your public reputation wouldn't help your case," Shirley said.

Naylor thought about what they'd said, then nodded and sat down at the counter.

"Okay, I guess you're right," he said. "But as soon as you get what you need on tape, you'll get out here, right?"

"Absolutely," Shirley said. "What time is it?"

"Five to seven," I said.

"We should probably head to the office," she said. "And let's get these dinner plates out of the way."

"Hang on," Bill said, reaching for the Dolmades. "Let me grab a couple more of these. They're fantastic."

"Good luck," I said, squeezing Naylor's hand.

Bill and Shirley headed for the office, but I walked to the wall of windows and peeked through the closed blinds.

"What are you doing?" Naylor said, walking toward me.

"Just checking on the peanut gallery," I said, looking across the street into Jennifer's window.

Josie and Chef Claire, along with Max and Jennifer, were sitting in the living room staring out the window.

"What are they doing?" Naylor said.

"It looks like they're eating popcorn," I said.

"Unbelievable," he said, shaking his head.

"Sadly, it's not," I said, closing the gap in the blinds just as Naylor's intercom buzzed. "Okay, it's showtime."

I headed for the office where Bill and Shirley were standing between two of the Japanese screens in dim light. I stood next to them and cocked my head and listened closely as the door opened then closed. I heard a muffled exchange, then both voices became clear as they entered the living room.

"Where did you put the microphone?" I whispered.

"In the table lamp next to where they'll be sitting," Bill said.

"Good call."

"Shhh," Shirley whispered.

"So, John, you decided you needed another five hundred thousand," Wilma said, her voice sounding surprisingly confident.

"Well, Wilma, what can I say?" Naylor said, going for casual and just missing. "Times are tough. And you did try to kill me."

"I must say it's warmer in here than the place where you made me drop off the first payment."

"Yeah, I'm sorry about that," Naylor said. "I wasn't quite ready to reveal myself at the time."

"Am I the only one you're going after, or do you have compromising photos of the others?"

"What others?" Naylor said.

"Well played," I whispered. "Get her talking."

"Shhh," Shirley said, glancing over her shoulder at me.

"I have your camera and computer, remember?"

"What do you think of them?"

"The pictures?" Wilma said. "To tell you the truth, the only ones I found on your camera were a bunch of dog photos. Those are the ones Wags is going to use for their marketing campaign, right?"

"Yeah."

"I have to say they turned out great. Good looking bunch of dogs," Wilma said.

"She's right," I whispered with a grin. "They looked adorable."

"Shhh," Shirley said.

"I haven't had time to go through your computer," Wilma said. "But I will. I can't way to see your wonderful collection of blackmail photos."

"You didn't go through my computer?" Naylor said.

"I just told you, I haven't had time," Wilma said. "And I had to get all your stuff out of our loft before Victor stumbled onto it. But don't worry, it's all resting comfortably in my safe deposit box."

"That was probably a mistake on your part," Naylor said.

"I doubt it. You know, John, I've been thinking. Since I have all your photos, there really isn't any reason for me to pay you anything. And if I don't walk out of here with a full briefcase and the other half million I've already given you, my lawyer and I will be going through your computer then speaking with everyone else you've got compromising photos of. I'm sure they'll be more than happy to join me in a major class action lawsuit."

"I see," Naylor said.

"You certainly will, John," she said.

"No, I don't think so, Wilma," Naylor said. "You won't be going through my computer. Not that there's anything incriminating on it."

"What are you talking about?" Wilma said.

"My camera and computer were returned to me this afternoon," Naylor said. "Imagine my surprise."

"That's impossible," she said. "You're bluffing."

"The kid's good," I whispered.

"Will you please be quiet?" Bill whispered a bit too loudly.

"What was that?" Wilma said.

"What?" Naylor said.

"I heard something," Wilma said, her voice sharp.

"Oh, I've got the TV on in the bedroom," Naylor said. "Let me go turn it off."

"Smooth," I whispered.

The kid was good. Moments later, Naylor poked his head in the office.

"Would you people mind keeping it down in here?" he whispered.

"Sorry," I said. "Actually, it was Bill's fault."

"Hey, don't blame me," Bill said.

"Just knock it off," Shirley whispered. "Both of you."

"Thank you," Naylor said, nodding at Shirley before heading back to the living room.

"Thanks for throwing me under the bus," Bill whispered.

"Don't mention it."

"Okay, the TV's off," Naylor said from the living room.

"It sounded familiar," Wilma said. "What were you watching?"

"Just some bad cop show."

"Funny," I whispered.

"Yeah, the kid's got a sense of humor," Bill whispered.

"Shhh," Shirley said.

256

"I asked you if you were blackmailing other people, John."

"No, you're the only one being blackmailed, Wilma," Naylor said. "Nice tattoo by the way."

"You're such a pig."

"Yeah, if you believe the rumors. That had to hurt, right?"

"Absolutely," I whispered. "Big time."

"Will you please shut it?" Shirley whispered through clenched teeth.

"Of course, it hurt," Wilma said. "Big time."

"Told ya," I whispered.

"Where did you get your hands on another five hundred thousand that fast?" Naylor said.

"Victor gave it to me," Wilma said. "Can you believe that? He's such a generous man."

"But you still feel the need to cheat on him?" Naylor said.

I listened closely and thought I heard the sound of Wilma sobbing.

"I made some mistakes," Wilma said. "And as soon as this whole thing is over, I'm going to do everything I can to repair the damage I've done. I simply can't afford to lose Victor. And I want all those photos destroyed and need your word that this is the last time you'll be asking me for money."

"I'm positive it will be," Naylor said.

"Really?"

"There's no doubt about it. Just as long as you don't try to take another shot at killing me," Naylor said. "I want all of this to be over."

"A million bucks," Wilma said, exhaling loudly. "That was an expensive affair."

"Yeah, I hope he was worth it," Naylor said. "So, you liked the dog photos?"

"Great transition," I whispered.

"Yeah, it was," Shirley whispered.

"I really did," Wilma said. "It's just a pity you don't focus on that sort of work more often. You'd almost come across as a human being."

"Thanks for the compliment," Naylor said, flatly. "I did the photo shoot the day Melinda died."

I waited out another round of sobbing.

"It was supposed to be you," Wilma said.

"I know it was," Naylor said. "I was very lucky. Where did you get your hands on the poison?"

"I know a guy," Wilma said.

"I imagine you know lots of guys," Naylor said.

"That's a cheap shot, Naylor."

"Yes, it was," he said. "You took the access card to my place from Melinda's purse when she was at dinner with you and Victor, right?"

"How did you know that?"

"It's the only thing that makes sense. You'd need an access card to get in and out without having to kick the door in," Naylor said. "You took the key, made some excuse to leave for a while, then came over here and sprinkled the powder on my pillow. It was a brilliant plan."

"But you didn't come home that night, did you?"

"No, I stayed at my girlfriend's place. So, the bed was untouched. Then after the photo shoot with the dogs was over, I headed out to run a few errands while Melinda took a nap. You must have been watching my place that morning and thought everyone had left."

Wilma started sobbing louder.

"And you still had Melinda's access card and had to get in here to take my equipment you couldn't find the night before," Naylor said. "But you saw her in the bedroom, didn't you?"

Wilma's crying was now interspersed with what sounded like soft howls.

"So, you panicked, put the access card back in her purse and grabbed my camera and computer, then got out of here as fast as you could. You left in such a hurry, you didn't even bother to close the door all the way."

"Ask her the question," I whispered.

"What question?" Shirley whispered.

"How did you get past security?" Naylor said.

"That one," I whispered.

"I told them I was visiting my friend on the eighth floor," Wilma said, sniffling. "They're used to seeing me around."

"The little tramp," Shirley whispered.

"Yeah," I said. "I feel bad for Victor."

"He's lucky he found out now," Bill whispered.

"I can't believe I'm responsible for killing that wonderful girl," Wilma said.

"Okay," Naylor said, loudly. "I think I'm done here."

"What are you talking about?" Wilma said.

"That's our cue," Bill said. "Let's go."

"One at a time going through the screens."

"What?" Shirley said, glancing over her shoulder.

"Nothing," I said, following her into the living room.

When Wilma saw us, her eyes grew wide, and she stood up and glanced back and forth at us.

"What's going on?" she said.

"We're just putting the final touches on a murder case," Bill said, positioning himself between Wilma and the front door.

"You set me up?" Wilma said, glaring at Naylor. "Getting a million dollars out of me wasn't enough?"

"Actually, Wilma," I said. "John hasn't tried to get one dollar out of you."

"What are you talking about?" she said, pointing at the briefcase. "What do you think is in that case?"

"I know exactly what's in the case," I said. "It was my idea."

"Your idea?" Wilma said, staring at me in disbelief.

"Yeah, somebody had to do it," I said, frowning. "Since Melinda isn't here to ask you for it."

Wilma stared at me for a very long time. Then she looked around the room trying to find the right words.

"Melinda was the one blackmailing me?" Wilma said.

I slowly nodded my head.

"Why would she do something like that? I was one of her favorite people in the whole world."

"Yes, I'm sure you were," I said. "And then you broke her heart when she saw you with Jeremiah in his loft. I imagine she felt that you betrayed her almost as much as you did Victor."

"She took the photos?" Wilma whispered.

"She did," Naylor said. "Right from those windows over there."

Stunned, Wilma slowly walked to the wall of windows and peered out through the blinds.

"I can't believe it," Wilma said. "I remember asking Jeremiah if we should close the curtains, but he laughed and asked me who on earth was going to be able to see us way up on the fourth floor. He's such an idiot."

Wilma stepped back from the windows and glanced around the loft.

"Okay," Bill said. "Let's do this."

"Are you ready to go, Wilma?" Shirley said, reaching for a pair of handcuffs.

"Yes, I think I am," Wilma whispered as her eyes darted around the loft. Then she made a beeline for the door that led out to the patio.

Shirley and Bill started after her and reached for their guns, but I held up a hand.

"No, it's okay," I said, just as the wind blew the door shut. "She's not going anywhere."

"Isn't there a fire escape out there?" Bill said.

"No, it's just one of those chain ladders," Naylor said. "And it's in a box. It would take her at least five minutes to set it up." He grinned at me. "That sounds about right, doesn't it, Suzy?"

"Shut it."

I flipped the switch that raised the blinds. Then I turned on the patio light, and we saw Wilma already hugging herself and hopping up and down for warmth as the snow and wind swirled around her. I glanced across the street into Jennifer's loft and saw Josie waving her phone. I grabbed my phone from my bag and called her.

"Hey," I said. "How's it going over there?"

"We're having a great time," Josie said. "But we didn't get a chance to watch any of the action with the blinds closed."

"Yeah, sorry about that," I said. "It couldn't be helped."

"Based on what I see on the patio, I'm gonna guess you guys got what you needed."

"We did."

"Are you coming over? Jennifer made an amazing antipasto. We're having Italian for dinner."

"Just as soon as I finish up here," I said, putting my phone away and glancing out at the patio. I looked at Bill and Shirley. "Aren't you guys going to go get her?"

"Nah, let's give her a few minutes," Bill said. "She's not going anywhere."

"Do you need us to stick around?" I said.

"No, you guys can leave," Shirley said. "We'll probably need to get statements from you, but that can wait."

"You'll make sure Victor gets his money back?" I said.

"We will," Bill said, nodding.

"Okay, then I think I'll get going," I said, then glanced at Naylor. "You ready?"

"I am," he said, grabbing his coat.

"You did good," I said.

"Thanks," he said. "But you wouldn't shut up."

"That was Bill," I said, grinning at the detective.

"Nice try," Bill said. "Thanks for all your help. You guys did great." Then he frowned when he saw the look on my face. "What's the matter?"

I pressed my hand against my forehead, then gently squeezed my throat.

"I think I'm coming down with something."

Epilogue

Not only did I come down with something, so did Josie and Chef Claire and Max. And we spent the next three days alternating between our bedrooms and his germ-infested living room in front of a roaring fire. When we weren't flat on our backs, we were coughing and sneezing and complaining while we pounded cold medicine and sipped hot toddies and reviewed the dog photos trying to decide which ones we'd be using in Wags' initial marketing campaign.

On the second day, after my fever broke, I was finally able to make my way to the living room around noon. I sat down near the fire and grimaced when Chloe hopped up on my lap. She stretched out and stared up at me with an expectant look on her face.

"Don't worry," I said with a phlegmy chuckle. "Mama will be just fine." I rubbed her head and blew my nose then sat back in the chair exhausted.

"This is all your fault," Josie said for about the hundredth time.

"You don't know that," I said, blowing my nose again. "Chef Claire was the one who went skiing three days in a row. She might have caught something."

"Don't blame me," Chef Claire said, tossing back a long swig of cold medicine straight from the bottle. "You were the one hanging out with cops who had the flu."

"Not to mention she also climbed down that ladder naked," Josie said. "That's a great way to catch a cold."

"The housekeeping uniform was just billowing in the wind," I snapped, then sneezed. "I wasn't naked."

"Maybe not," Josie said, with an evil grin. "But that's the way I'm going to be telling the story." She tried to laugh, then her head began to sway back and forth, and it looked like she was about to throw up. "I need to go back to bed."

"Good idea," Chef Claire said, draping a blanket over her shoulders and grabbing the bottle of cold medicine as she headed toward her room with a small wave.

I sat there by myself for a few minutes then decided bed was still the preferred option. I climbed in next to the sleeping Max. I turned my head and flipped onto my side and studied him until my eyes began to close. Just before I drifted off, I came to the conclusion that one's ability to lie next to a sweat-drenched snorer and be completely content was most definitely a sign of true love.

On the third day, we were back to about eighty percent and ready to make the drive home. We packed amid the bouncing and yapping of four excited dogs, then walked down the driveway rolling our bags behind us. The sun was out, and the snow left behind by the massive early-winter storm was starting to melt. I unlocked my SUV, and Max organized the bags in the back of the vehicle. Then he closed the back hatch and gave me a long hug and a kiss.

"I'll see you Wednesday afternoon," he said.

"I need to warn you that we're going to put you to work," Chef Claire said. "We'll be feeding a couple hundred people at the restaurant."

"You can help wash dishes," I said.

"I can do that," he said, then knelt down to pet all four dogs who were anxious to get on the road. "And I'll see you guys in a couple of days."

"Okay, Goofballs, let's go," Josie said, clapping her hands once.

All four dogs hopped into the car, and Captain and Chloe climbed over the backseat next to the suitcases and spent a few minutes selecting their spots. Chef Claire got in the back, and Al and Dente sat down on either side of her.

"Crowded back there?" Max said, glancing through the back window and laughing.

"It's cozy," Chef Claire said, draping her arms over both Goldens.

"Drive safe," Max said, leaning in through the driver side window. "And call me when you get home."

"Will do," I said, giving him a final kiss. "Thanks for everything. And I promise the next time I visit there won't be any dead bodies.

Josie snorted and pulled out a fresh bag of bite-sized.

I waved goodbye and drove down the driveway out onto the bare street and headed for the highway that would take us home.

Home.

I was more than ready.

About a half-hour later, my phone buzzed, and I placed it in its dashboard holder and put it on speaker.

"This is Suzy," I said, moving into the slow lane.

"Hey, it's me."

"Victor," I said, surprised. "I've been meaning to give you a call, but we all got sick."

"Yeah, I heard," he said. "Bill and Shirley told me."

"What's up?"

"You'll never guess what the cops just found," Victor said.

"A nine-millimeter and some spare change in the seat cushions of their couch?"

"Yeah, good one," he said. "They found the first five hundred thousand that Wilma paid Melinda."

"Really? Where was it?"

"It was under the mattress," Victor said.

"She put it under her bed?" I said, frowning as I remembered the condition of her apartment and the sketchy neighborhood it was located in.

"No, it was under our bed. Bill and Shirley were here taking a look around. My housekeeper asked them to help her flip the mattress, and there it was."

267

"That makes no sense," I said, glancing over at Josie.

"But it's one heck of an early Christmas present," Josie said.

"Oh, hi, Josie," Victor said. "How are you doing?"

"Finally able to sit up and take nourishment," she said, sniffling.

"Thanks for the warning," he deadpanned.

"Funny," Josie said, reaching for a bite-sized.

"Melinda felt guilty and gave the money back?" I said.

"It looks that way," Victor said. "But none of it makes any sense."

"What are you going to do with it?" I said.

"I'm sure most of it will end up going for bail and to Wilma's lawyers," he said, rattling his ice cubes.

"Have you talked to her?"

"No, she's convinced that I was the one who set her up with the cops. Which is partly true, right?"

"Yeah, I guess it is," I said, shrugging. "The two of you are officially done?"

"We are."

"I'm sorry, Victor."

"Don't be," he said, rattling his ice again.

"Victor," I said, annoyed. "Please don't do that."

"Sorry."

"Say, why don't you drive down and spend Thanksgiving with us?"

"Hey, that's not a bad idea," he said. "I might just do that."

"We're going to have two seatings at the restaurant. The second one is going to start around four. You should come. We'll put you to work."

"I'll let you know," he said. "Say, how did the photos turn out?"

"They look great," I said. "And Naylor is coming for Thanksgiving and bringing some of the mockups with him. One more reason to drop by."

"Yeah, that sounds good. I gotta run," he said, giving his ice cubes one final rattle next to the phone before ending the call.

"She gave the money back?" Josie said, frowning at me.

"Maybe she was just trying to make a point," I said.

"The point being I'm a total nut job?" Chef Claire said from the backseat.

"Weird," I said, shaking my head. "In that poem, she said that five hundred notes won't kill the pain."

"What about it?" Josie said.

"I originally thought it was a reference that the five hundred grand wasn't enough money. But maybe she was talking about how money, regardless of the amount, could never make up for the loss she felt. And maybe that's why she gave the money back."

"Interesting. But who was the gray voyeur?" Josie said. "I don't get that one."

"Me either," I said, glancing over at her.

"Melinda was the gray voyeur," Chef Claire said.

"I'm going to need a bit more," I said, glancing at her through the rearview mirror.

"Me too," Josie said, turning around in her seat.

"Gray is a reference to her mood. Not hair color. When things stop being black and white, they often turn gray," Chef Claire said. "And she was probably talking to herself in the mirror throughout that poem. It's a self-reflection piece."

I glanced at Josie who eventually nodded, impressed.

"That's pretty good," she said to Chef Claire.

"It's amazing," I said. "How the heck did you figure that out?"

"I have my moments," Chef Claire said with a shrug.

We made it home just before five and headed straight for the Inn. The dogs flew out of the SUV and raced to the front door and barked at us to hurry up. The reception area was empty, and Sammy and Jill entered from the condo area.

"Hey, you made it," Jill said, heading toward us then coming to a stop a few feet away. "Are you guys still contagious?"

"No, we're good," Josie said, reaching out to give both of them hugs. "No thanks to Suzy."

I made a face at her then turned back to Sammy and Jill.

"Is everything okay?"

"Things are great," Sammy said. "We just fed and watered the gang, and they're about to head out to take care of their business."

"Thanks, guys," I said, glancing back and forth at them.

"Yeah, great job," Josie said. "Why don't we go say hi to the dogs, then head up to the house?"

"Perfect," I said, glancing around. "It's so nice to be home."

"It is," Chef Claire said. "How about I take the bruisers up to the house and get started on dinner?"

"What are you gonna make?" Josie said, cocking her head at Chef Claire.

"Josie, you haven't eaten a solid meal in three days. Is it really going to matter what I make?"

"Good point."

After two days of hanging around the house with the dogs, we were finally fully-recovered and ready for Thanksgiving. We headed to the restaurant just after six in the morning, and Chef Claire put us to work immediately chopping vegetables for side dishes and the stuffing. By nine, the kitchen was filled with a wide range of amazing smells and Josie and I had to fight hard to maintain our concentration. By noon, the dining room was packed with local residents, and we stood behind the buffet table watching and listening to the hum of the conversations interspersed with laughter.

"This is nice," I said, glancing over at Josie.

"It is," she said, reaching for a slice of turkey before looking around the crowded dining room. "I think it's my favorite day of the year. And not just because there's a ton of food."

"I know what you mean," I said, then saw my mother and Paulie heading our way. "Hey, Mom. Paulie. Happy Thanksgiving."

"Same to you, darling," my mother said, giving both of us hugs and kisses on the cheek.

"Are you ready to eat?"

"No, we're going to wait for the second seating," she said. "But we thought we'd stop by early to help out."

"You have your choice of serving dessert or helping Max with dishes in the kitchen," I said.

My mother glanced over at Paulie with a small smile.

"I'll be in the kitchen with Max if you're looking for me," he said, heading off.

"There are John and Jennifer," I said, waving to the couple who were standing at the entrance to the dining room.

I eventually caught their eye, and they headed straight for us.

"You made it," I said. "Mom, this is John Naylor."

"It's nice to meet you, John," she said, shaking his hand. "How have you been, Jennifer?"

"I'm doing very well, Mrs. C.," she said, giving my mother a long hug. "You look fantastic. As always."

"You're too kind. I hope all that nasty business you had to deal with is finally settling down," my mother said.

"Yes, it is," Jennifer said, squeezing Naylor's hand.

"I smell a comeback," my mother said.

"I don't know if it's a comeback," Jennifer said. "But something sure smells good."

"Would you like to eat now or wait for the second seating?" I said.

"I think we're going to wait," Jennifer said, then whispered something in Naylor's ear.

He smiled and nodded, and they headed for the lounge waving as they walked off.

"Mom," I whispered, leaning in close to my mother.

"Yes, darling?"

"Is there anybody you don't know?"

"Oh, I'm sure there must be, right?" she deadpanned, then glanced at me and laughed.

By the time the second seating was over, we had all eaten way too much, and after we said goodbye to our guests, we headed for the lounge to relax with our inner circle. Jackson, our former chief of police, was talking with Chief Abrams, our current chief, and Freddie, our local medical examiner. But instead of talking crime, they were arguing about football and watching the night game that was displayed on the screens that ringed the bar and lounge area. Max was sitting at the bar next to our good friend Rooster who was regaling my boyfriend with way too many stories about me in my younger days.

"Wonderful job, ladies," my mother said, patting my hand. "You made a lot of people very happy today."

"We love doing it, Mrs. C.," Chef Claire said.

"Absolutely," Josie said, getting up from her chair. "I'm going to duck home and grab the dogs. It looks like we'll be here for a while and they've been alone all day."

"Great idea," Chef Claire said. "I'll give you a hand."

"No, you just sit there and relax," Josie said. "You've done way more than enough work for one day. I'll be right back."

We watched her leave, then my mother leaned in close.

"I take it things are still going well with you and Max," she said.

"Unbelievably well," I said, glancing over at the bar.

"Good," she said, nodding. "I like him a lot."

"Me too," I said, then glanced up when our bar manager, Millie, arrived holding three snifters that were steaming hot.

"Rooster sent these over for you," she said, setting the snifters down in front of us.

"B&B, right?" I said, reaching for mine.

"Yes. And microwaved for twenty seconds," she said. "I thought Rooster was nuts when he asked me to do it, but it tastes amazing."

"Thanks, Millie," Chef Claire said. "And thanks for agreeing to be here all day. We really appreciate it."

"Are you kidding?" she said, laughing. "It's the best party in town. Now, if you'll excuse me, there's a big glass of Pinot over there with my name on it."

"Did you guys get enough to eat?" I said, glancing over at John and Jennifer.

"Trick question, right?" John said, shifting in his chair to get comfortable. "I was going to show you the mockups tonight, but I don't think I can move. Let's do it tomorrow, okay?"

"That's fine," I said, fighting the fumes and taking a sip of B&B. "Did you get a chance to take a look at Melinda's journal?"

"I did," he said, giving me a sad smile. "It's amazing. I'd like to do the book as a tribute to her."

"Nice. You're a good man, John."

"Don't spread it around," he said, squeezing Jennifer's hand. "You'll ruin my reputation as a total sleazeball."

A few minutes later, Josie returned with the four dogs leading the way. They all said hello to everyone then Chloe started to jump up on my lap. I gently stopped her, then she sat down at my feet, and I rubbed her head.

"Mama is going to need a few minutes to digest," I said.

Chloe stretched out over my feet then started wrestling with Captain on the floor.

"Okay, Goofball," Josie said to Captain. "Settle down."

The Newfie softly woofed at her, then stretched out over her feet. Josie rubbed his head then gently thumped his side as he stared at John and Jennifer.

"Look at him," Jennifer said, shaking her head. "He's magnificent."

"Thanks," Josie said. "He is pretty special."

Captain woofed again in agreement.

"Hey, I almost forgot," Naylor said, reaching into his bag. "I had these made up."

He held up a long red scarf that was emblazoned with the Wags logo in green.

"I thought these would look great for our Christmas ads," he said. "We can grab some shots of the dogs wearing them tomorrow."

"How cute," I said, reaching for the scarf and tying it around Chloe's neck.

"That's adorable," my mother cooed.

"I got four of them," Naylor said, tossing two of them to Chef Claire. "But since Captain is going to refuse to wear his, I guess you guys will have an extra one."

"Look at that," Chef Claire said, beaming at Al and Dente who were very pleased with their new scarves.

"Oh, those pictures are going to be so cute," I said.

We spent the next few minutes fawning over the three dogs, then Captain wandered over to Naylor and nudged his arm.

"Well, what do you know?" Josie said, laughing.

Captain looked up at Naylor and woofed.

"Would you like a scarf, Captain?" Naylor said.

Captain woofed again, this time a little louder. Naylor draped the remaining scarf around the dog's neck then tied it. The Newfie turned, then sat down and posed for the group.

"The Natty Newfie," Naylor said, laughing.

"I'm ready for my closeup, Mr. DeMille," Josie deadpanned.

"Unbelievable. I think he likes it," I said, shaking my head. "Who's ready for another drink?"

Several hands went up, and I waved everyone back into their seats.

"No, sit. I'll get them," I said.

"I'll give you a hand," Josie said.

I came up behind Max and nuzzled his neck.

"Having fun?"

"Yeah, I'm having a fantastic time. Rooster was just telling me about the time you fell out of the boat when you guys were fishing."

"Yeah, not my finest moment," I said, frowning.

"But it was definitely one of your funniest," Rooster said.

"Not even close," Josie said. "You should have seen her on the ladder the other night swaying in the breeze."

Max snorted midway through a sip of B&B. He coughed and wiped his mouth, laughing the entire time.

"Shut it. Both of you."

"You guys need another round over there?" Millie said.

"Yes, please," I said, glancing up at the one TV that didn't have the football game on. I stared at the screen and realized I was looking at a breaking news story. "Hey, Millie. Could you please turn the volume up on that one?"

"You're going to watch Canadian news?" Max said, glancing back at me.

"It looks like there's been some sort of accident," I said, staring up at the screen.

"Earlier this evening, about thirty miles off the coast of Saint Thomas in the U.S. Virgin Islands, police responded to a distress call from a sailboat named The Widow Maker. Police are now reporting that Charlotte Evans, noted Ottawa socialite, apparently drowned tonight after she inexplicably decided to go for a late-night swim in shark-infested waters. She and her husband, George Theo, the well-known Canadian mining magnate, were on their honeymoon at the time of the accident. Mr. Theo, who was asleep below deck at the time of his wife's ill-fated swim, made the distress call after he realized his wife of two days was missing. Given the late hour, Island police and the Coast Guard won't be able to begin their search of the area until morning. When asked about the chances for a successful rescue, a police representative responded by saying the odds weren't in their favor."

"That's cop-speak for slim and none," I said, grabbing the remote and lowering the volume.

"Yeah," Josie said. "Hey, didn't you say that George told you he was the best man at her last wedding?"

"Yup," I said, nodding. "Her fifth husband was his best friend." I took a sip of my B&B as I looked back up at the screen. "George, you little devil."

"What?" Max said, glancing over his shoulder.

"Nothing. It's not important."